MUST LOVE SILENCE

LUCY BEXLEY

Credits:

Cover design by Lucy Bexley

Cover photo by Jr Korpa on Unsplash

Edited by Amanda Laufhutte

SYNOPSIS

Reese Walker doesn't like people. What she likes is silence and being left alone. The thing she loves most about recording audiobooks is that she doesn't have to leave her Chicago apartment to do it. And she hasn't for nearly a year. But with an unavoidable bill going to collections that puts her sister's treatment at risk, she has no choice but to take a job that pushes her out of her comfort zone.

After a disastrous blow to her career, Arden Abbott needs a comeback. Step one: a successful book launch, including an audiobook. She doesn't trust anyone else to oversee every aspect of the project. It has to be flawless. Arden knows she's ready to resume the life she had before her dreams fell apart, all she has to do is prove it to everyone around her.

When Reese and Arden meet, sparks fly and then they combust. Will Reese crack under the constant pressure from Arden? Can she possibly read a sex scene with the woman who wrote it interrupting to correct her pronunciation of words she is saying 100% correctly? Or can they step outside their comfort zones long enough to meet in the middle...

Must Love Silence is an enemies-to-lovers slow burn workplace lesbian romance featuring a lovable misanthrope and a heroine in recovery. It's funny and a little dark, and it firmly believes that everyone deserves a chance to change.

This book is for everyone who wants therapists to laugh at their jokes.

I've had some success with this by marrying one.

ONE

Reese snapped on her headphones like a pilot readying for takeoff. The soft thud of the foam against her ears took the fake opera assaulting her from an eleven down to a manageable six. Her next-door neighbor, Judith, could invade her apartment without even stepping inside. It was auditory warfare.

Her vocal exercises filled the room as she prepared for her day of recording. What would it cost to soundproof her entire apartment, rather than just her studio? The sooner she finished these chapters, the sooner she'd get paid. And the sooner she got paid, the sooner she could order that glass and wood coffee maker that looked like something out of an 18th-century apothecary lab that she'd had her eye on.

She wasn't sure how long the knocking had been going on for before she noticed it. At first, she caught a tremor in the door, a blurry vibration like a heatwave emanating from the highway. Reese thought about ignoring it—no one ever came here, and she never left. It was probably one of Judith's many loud visitors, here for another night of cards.

She held her headphones away from her ears for a moment, still intending to just wait them out until Judith intercepted them.

"Reese Walker, I know you're in there. I heard you talking." The gruff voice was like sandpaper on her ears. She resisted the urge to pull her headphones back up and block out this unpleasantness.

Shit. How did a stranger know her name? Had he really heard her reciting Ice, Ice, Baby like a Shakespearean sonnet? Some people might consider that an honor, but it's a privilege that's earned.

Reese tiptoed to the door, holding her breath. Her lungs burned as she looked out the viewfinder into the hall. The rather sweaty, magenta-colored face of a man who looked like he meant business greeted her. His slate-blue post office issue jacket was a size too small and strained at the shoulders in protest. Above his mouth, a gray mustache sat like a push broom, obscuring his expression. Such a fine line between a smile and a snarl. From the aggression of his knocking, she assumed it was grim.

Reese might not like people, but she respected delivery guys. *Delivery people*—no need to gender it. Mostly, she liked the ladies. She often left cookies out for them because she viewed them as modern-day Santas bringing her useless toys and also the kind of clutch packages you only appreciate as an adult, like wool socks and gift cards. But this Santa seemed as far from jolly as the South Pole is from the North.

She saw him raise his fist and flinched back from the door just before he made contact, assaulting her ears with a machine-gun rhythm.

There was no law that said she had to answer the door for the post office. It's not like he could break it down to make her sign for a package. Right? Companies had been getting a lot more rights ever since they became people.

"Ms. Walker. I need you to open the door and sign for this. I can't leave until you do. Or I will be forced to come back every single day."

Reese held her breath. Would tomorrow be better for her? Right now, it seemed a hell of a lot better than today.

"I can see your feet under the door."

Reese took another step back. She wanted him to be bluffing. She heard a door creak open and knew from the high-pitched squeal of the hinges that cyclone Judith was about to get involved.

Fuck. The very last thing she needed was Judith any more involved in her life.

Reese took a deep breath and set about unbolting the three locks and a single chain securing her door. She threw the door to the hall open and leaned against the frame, running a hand through her hair and leaving it a bit tousled.

"Sorry about that," she said pointing to the headphones hanging around her neck like earmuffs, "I didn't hear you at first."

"That must be some music you're listening to. Look, I need you to sign for this then I can be on my way."

"It's white noise." Reese glanced around the door and saw Judith tipping into the hall. Judith caught her eye and *waved*. The audacity. "What am I signing for?"

"It's a certified letter. The sender paid for proof of delivery."

What a waste. Who even opens mail? "And how do I know it's not bad news?"

"In my experience, these letters are rarely good news. But you're still required to accept it."

"Fine, do you have a pen?" Reese held out her hand as he pinched a ballpoint from his jacket pocket.

Reese kept her feet in her apartment and leaned into the hallway like the threshold was lava as she scribbled her name on the slip. She never stepped into the hall if she could help it, not since the great Judith incident of January 2019, when she'd screamed "fire" at three am. Reese had shot out of her apartment braless and breathless clutching her delicate aloe plant as she fled down to the street below. Judith was there waiting in the ugliest and pinkest robe she'd ever seen. She found out later that the fire was just a burnt smell coming from Judith's oven after she'd forgotten about some oatmeal raisin cookies. The raisins were strike one—a clear violation. Never again would she evacuate before she could both smell and taste the smoke. Hell was other people, notably Judith.

The postman handed over the letter and her stomach dropped when she saw the return address. Serenity Sobriety and Recovery in Detroit.

Reese thanked the man and closed the door, but before the latch caught, another knock came. Had she not signed everywhere she needed to?

The door creaked back open, protesting when Judith surged forward like a Black Friday shopper desperate for a stand mixer.

"Reese, glad to see you're still alive, my dear. I was beginning to wonder."

"Hi, Judith," Reese said as she straightened up, slipping the letter into her back pocket.

"What was that all about? You don't usually have visitors."

"You know as much as I do—you were watching from

two feet away," Reese said. She immediately felt annoyed with herself for the bite in her voice. She felt eager to open the bill, but under no circumstances would she open up that part of her life to Judith—she'd probably ask a lot of questions, or worse, try to help. "Anyway, how have you been?" Reese raised her voice at the end mimicking a cheerful person asking a question as though they were interested in the answer.

"I'm good—canasta club tonight. Any interest in joining? I could ask Sally to bring her daughter. I heard from Annalynn that she dated a woman after her divorce." Judith shoved her hands into the pockets of her white silk pajama pants. Her peony pink silk robe was pinched around her waist and it matched perfectly the pink foam rollers spiking out of her hair, like a head full of Easter eggs poorly hidden in dead grass.

"I'm good, thanks. Lots of work to do."

"You work too much. I hear you practicing those sexy readings on your fire escape sometimes. Do you really get paid to make those noises?"

Reese truly wished the hallway was lava so she could swan dive into it and escape this conversation forever.

"I get paid, but not very well," Reese's smile was a grimace in drag.

"Well, you love it, that's what matters! And you sound like you could make a lucky lady very happy one day. But I'm not sure how you plan to fall in love if you never leave this apartment of yours. I'm just trying to bring the options to you, dear."

"I don't want to fall in love, Judith. People are terrible." Reese could feel the letter burning in her back pocket. Jumping into that lava would probably solve several of her most pressing problems right now. The unpleasant singe would be nothing compared to this actual never-ending torture of discussing her queer love life with her 70-year-old neighbor. A neighbor who had not just overheard her practicing sex scenes for audiobooks but had actually *listened* enough to have opinions about her performance. She either wanted to end this conversation quickly or die trying.

"Not everyone is terrible."

"Name one person that isn't."

"Well, me!" Judith said with a chuckle as Reese fought to keep her face blank. "And I don't for one second believe you're terrible either. People are good at heart, and a lot of us want the best for you. We'd help if you'd let us!"

"Thanks, Judith. Let's agree to disagree on that one. I've met people; they aren't good."

"Well, not all people are good maybe, but most. You're shutting the good ones out with the bad, like throwing the baby out with the bathwater. Save the baby, Reese." Judith's laugh was the wheeze of bellows fanning the flames of Reese's smoldering rage. "You should give Sally's daughter a chance! She's probably not terrible. I mean Sally gossips a little too much for my taste, and I hear her daughter can be a bit of a handful, and the way she goes through women, my God. Anyway, just think about it. You could use a little excitement—you don't have to be soulmates."

"Ok, that's good to know. Look I really have to get to work now—those scenes won't record themselves. Have a good day, Judith."

Reese took a step backward into her apartment. She watched with alarm as Judith took a half step forward as though she might try to breach the threshold. Something she didn't even like her sister doing.

"Just let me know about la—"

Reese grimaced as she shut the door on Judith's frantically hopeful face. "Ok, Judith, I'll let you know!" she said, raising her voice to carry through the barrier. She'd never been more grateful for an ancient slab of oak. Did she feel bad about closing the door on Judith? Absolutely. Did she have to be rude to save herself? Also, yes. She'd learned a long time ago that if she didn't shut the door *and* lock it, Judith would walk right in, kick off her house shoes, and start prepping a hot dish.

Bolting the door, Reese slumped against it as her heart rate prepared for landing. Less than three minutes with Judith and she craved a nap.

Reese pulled the envelope from her back pocket cradling it on her palms. She set it down on the table and filleted it open with her paring knife. She shook the envelope and let the guts of the letter spill out onto the table. She pinched the edges gingerly, her eyes skipped down the page reading only what was bolded. Even bills had filler these days.

A final overdue notice—strange because she hadn't seen any other notices. Which might have something to do with the stack of unopened mail she kept by the door. She quite liked the look of it—it reminded her of baklava. Serious mail should come in red envelopes, although unless it also exploded, it probably would take its place in the stack all the same.

Her eyes came to rest on the bottom of the page. Overdue in the amount of $22,000, which was $2,000 more than the original cost of treatment. Fees and interest should be illegal.

At the bottom of the page in angry red letters was the threat: payment due upon receipt, but no later than 14 days from delivery of the letter otherwise the account would go to collections. *Shit.* She knew she shouldn't have signed that slip. Nothing good ever came from answering her door. Not one good thing. Now she was on the hook for $22,000 that she absolutely, 100% didn't have. Her dream of the beautiful coffee contraption that was going to solve all of her problems and make her happy forever shattered into a million glittering pieces. But what was the worst they could do, really? Would the rehab center really send a collections agency after her? Or would they simply send another letter with even larger, even redder font?

Reese continued reading, "Furthermore, failure to pay by the due date would result in termination of treatment."

Well, that was pretty bad as absolute catastrophes went. A very dramatic image of her sister, Lauren, being put out onto the street like some kind of Dickensian urchin flashed through her mind. Never mind that Lo was 34 and not as helpless as the drinking sometimes made her seem. She had a law degree, not that she was allowed to use it anymore.

How had she messed this up so badly? She knew Lo had put her payment information down when she checked into rehab this time. She had blindly agreed to cover the costs. She would have agreed to anything to get Lo out of her bad relationship and sober again. She'd been so busy avoiding the mail and everything else that she'd nearly cost her sister her recovery. Selfish and reckless.

How was she going to come up with that kind of money or anything close to it in two weeks? She could sell a kidney but that would probably require leaving her apartment, which made it a less attractive option. She had the money coming in from her most recent job, assuming she could finish recording today. Plus, she could drain her savings, but that still left her short and with no money for incidentals, like her own food or rent.

Reese picked up her phone and dialed the only number she could think of, her only in-case-of-emergency.

"Hello, this is David Remmer."

"Well, hello Mr. Professional Robot."

"Reesy! I was wondering when you were going to call me back."

"Oh right. You called." Reese tried to keep the confusion out of her voice.

"And you didn't notice. I'll pretend like that isn't a sledgehammer to my ego."

"Wow, a little dramatic."

"I learned from the best. Queen Reesey, first of her name, hater of all her subjects."

"You know it's not personal. All calls except Lo's go straight to voicemail and I check those when I can."

"Which is never."

"Which is never. Correct. So, what were you calling about?"

"I just wanted to check on you and on Lo. Is she doing ok? Adam says she's making good progress."

"Funny you should bring that up. I just opened a pretty hefty bill from the rehab. I may have inadvertently missed the first few."

"Reese, I love you, but you know I had to call in a favor with him to get Lo in on such short notice."

"I know. And I'm going to pay for it. Actually, speaking of desperately needing money I was wondering if you had any jobs I could do? I'll take anything—nonfiction, even heteromance."

"I'm surprised you were able to say that without throwing up."

"Hey, I know heterosexual people have sex, it's just not something I like to think about."

"I missed the way you say heterosexual like it's two separate words and you don't like either of them."

Reese laughed. "I guess I do. Look, I recorded my share of straight romances when I first started out, they just require a lot more acting, much like my straight relationships in high school did."

"Well, you definitely had to act a lot with Justin. That guy was as interesting as a tapeworm."

"Kissed like one, too."

"Please don't ever tell me things like that. I just threw up a little."

"Ok, focus. I'm kind of freaking out about this money thing."

"Oh, right, sorry. Ok, so there is this one job, but I don't think you'll want it."

"I already told you I'll record a straight romance."

"It's not that, it's a lesbian romance, it's just—"

"That's perfect! I'll do it."

"Well, I can definitely get you an audition."

"Can you just send my samples? Or send me the scenes and I'll record them today."

"Oh, sweet, naive, introverted Reese. Are you familiar with Arden Abbott?"

"Of course, she's big time. She's written, what, 15 books? All of them best-sellers."

"Let me rephrase. Are you familiar with Arden Abbott's reputation as a person?"

"Hopefully I'm about to be."

"Ok, just remember you said that. So, her audiobook narrator just dropped out, she says she's in the hospital with laryngitis. Who knows, maybe she is. She's looking for a replacement to start in the next few days, but first, you'd need to audition."

"That's pretty standard. Can you send me the scenes today?"

"Ms. Abbott likes a cold audition."

"What does that mean? Like over video call? Or she wants me to be physically cold? I guess I could record on my fire escape."

"You're hilarious," David said drily. "So glad your hibernation hasn't taken that away from you. Cold like cold open —in person in New York. She's a bit exacting, but hey, I guess you don't reach her level of success without a few control issues."

"Hmm." She was incapable of forming a professional response to that.

"Listen, before you say no, don't say no."

"I'm sorry, are you telling me I'd need to fly to New York to talk to myself in a room all day when I have a perfectly good converted linen closet in my apartment?"

"Well, you wouldn't be by yourself, actually. I'm doing production, for one."

"And for two?"

"And she likes to oversee the entire process."

"Meaning?"

"She's there for the recording sessions. In the studio. Sometimes she gives notes."

"I don't think I can do that, David. She'd what? Make eye contact with me while I read sex scenes she wrote and then critique my breathy moans? Judith already has that covered."

"How is Judith by the way?"

"Not now. I don't think I'd make enough to even cover my travel expenses. And I doubt I'd get hazard pay to compensate for that trauma." Her body shuddered with the violence of a phone on a coffee table.

"Did I mention that everyone loved the files you sent last week? The entire team is really pleased with your work on *Away with Me*. I heard a married straight woman dreamily call your voice 'smoky.'"

"Glad to hear all the pot is finally paying off," Reese said, dropping her voice an octave into a husky laugh.

"Speaking of paying off, I think I could negotiate your pay to double your usual rate if Ms. Abbott likes your audition."

The wheels started to turn; she was already getting nearly double her regular rate for *Away with Me*, her first audiobook for a major publisher. And double that would get her very close to paying off Lo's rehab in full, no bartering or IOUs needed, just good ol' American legal tender.

"Where's the studio again?"

"Ah ha, I knew the money would draw you in. The studio is in Brooklyn. I know you'd have to leave your apartment *but* just think about the bagels. And the pizza."

"Detroit-style pizza for life, Davey, how could you?" Reese injected her voice with the same dramatic shock she used when a fictional cheating spouse was exposed.

"That's not pizza, that's a casserole," David said indignantly. "Please don't tell your father I said that."

"Ok, you've got me. I'll think about it and get back to you."

"I'd actually need a yes today, and you'd need to be on the first flight out tomorrow morning to audition. Ms. Abbott's been very clear that the timeline can't budge, and she's not willing to extend the studio booking, so you'd have a little under two weeks to record the novel start-to-finish."

"Is this a thing? This calling her Ms. Abbott? Isn't she our age?"

"She's a few years older, early 30s, I think. I call her Ms. Abbott out of fear and respect."

"Ok fine, I'll go to New York. But I'm only doing it because I want to see you, and I really want one of those street-corner pretzels."

"And the money, don't forget about that."

"How could I ever forget about that?"

TWO

The plane Reese should have been on disappeared into the clear blue sky without her. A blender full of relief and anxiety churned in her stomach—one tumbling over the other until they became a terrible smoothie.

To put it mildly, she was freaking the hell out. Most opportunities were a mistake. Everyone knew that. You regret 100% of the chances you take. When God closes a door, he opens a window for you to fall out of. No way she could survive a fall from a mile high. Much better to risk falling off her own reasonably high fire escape where she had a chance of landing in the dumpster below.

Reese had to get on the next tin can death trap to New York, and she also absolutely could not do that. The decision sat heavily on her shoulders, dragging her down. She shifted her bag to her other arm.

Going for this job was a horrible, no good, very bad, totally necessary idea and Reese hated it. Who knew what the future held? She could spend the next two hours sitting next to a man who hogged the armrest and spat while he talked at her about deer season, and at the end of that odyssey *still* not get this job. Sure, getting this paycheck could solve all her problems, but at what cost?

The airport buzzed around the edges of her headphones and muffled everything in a pleasant underwater way. A sharp bump to her shoulder sent her stumbling forward, and a man in a Hawaiian shirt shuffled by, his flip-flops swooshing across the linoleum. She looked down at her own leather jacket and boots—she was in another season entirely. She'd forgotten airports were always everything at once, each gate a mini Epcot diorama, except here the food was worse. Probably.

She felt something move against her ass, and she spun around ready to swat the offending intrusion. But there was no one behind her—neither man nor mosquito, just her phone buzzing again right where she'd left it in her back pocket. What a strange sensation. She couldn't remember the last time she'd worn pants with pockets, let alone felt her phone demand her attention like some grabby dude at a bar.

She didn't recognize the number on the screen, and she let her finger hover over the dismiss button. Guilt at missing the flight she hadn't paid for to go to a meeting that could change her life compelled her to answer, and she hit accept before she could fully process the change in protocol.

"Hello, this is Reese." She slipped into her reading voice.

"Reese? Where are you? Are you on the fire escape? Your voice sounds deeper."

Unbelievable. She'd just wasted her professional voice on Judith. Judith's words were more rapid than normal, as if she'd just scaled the side of the building looking for Reese. Maybe she had.

"Hi Judith, is the building on fire?" Why in the hell hadn't she saved Judith's number as one of her DO NOT ANSWERs. Rookie mistake.

"What? No, I don't think so. I came by to tell you about canasta and drop off some leftover cake, but you're not answering your door. I've been knocking and knocking. I almost called 911. Are you sick? Are you hurt?"

"I'm fine." Reese breathed out deeply, pushing her anxiety away from her like a car into a lake, a great heave that took everything she had. She watched all her problems sink below the surface of the conversation with a gurgling protest. Judith would latch on to the slightest tremor in her voice and stage a horrifying golf cart rescue through the airport in minutes. "I have to go out of town for work."

Silence crackled on the line. Reese raised her phone hoping the terrible airport reception had done her a solid and dropped the call, but the call timer was still ticking.

"Did I lose you, Judith?"

"No, I thought I heard you say you're going out of town for work, and I had to sit down. I think I'm hallucinating. I knew there was something off with that spin dip last night. Don't worry, those aren't the leftovers I brought you."

"You're not hallucinating. I got a job... interview, so I'll be gone for a few days to a few weeks depending on whether they like me. And I can't take the leftovers, I'm not home."

"Well, if you're reading a kissing book, how could they not love you? You're a pro. I've listened to every book you've done. That nice librarian Susie showed me how to search you and then download audiobooks onto my phone. Do you know Susie? She's pretty quiet, maybe you two could date?"

"I'm looking for more in a relationship than someone not talking to me."

"Oh, like what?" Judith's voice squeaked, and Reese could picture her with a pen poised over a bright pink notepad ready to make a list.

"Thanks for checking on me, Judith. I really should get going though—I'm about to board." Reese looked at the empty gate. The next flight to New York had just posted, and she needed to grovel for her shot at three hours of forced proximity and cocktail peanuts.

"Ok, I don't want to bother you, dear. Not with your important business flight—this is so exciting! Is there anything I can do for you while you're away?"

She couldn't remember the last time someone offered to help her with something, she had a flash of warmth in her chest. Usually she was helping Lo with some crisis. She heard Judith inhale deeply over the line, and the warmth dissipated. She knew that preparatory inhale. Shit.

"I could get your mail! Or did you have a chance to clean out your fridge before you left? Or maybe I could help with laundry? You know I've got a sewing machine and I've been practicing my hemming. I could alter some of your clothes for you. I noticed you had cuffed the jeans you were wearing the other day. Are they too long? Taking them up an inch would fix that right up."

The cool sting of airport air conditioning stung her wide eyes. If hell was still working on the circle system, Judith touching her clothes was the fifth circle at least. She spun through a mental rolodex of tasks that Judith could do, looking for the least invasive. Anything to redirect the conversation. She knew if she didn't toss Judith a soft ball she'd come back to a closet full of capris and her perfect, blank walls covered in floral wallpaper like a rose garden with motion sickness.

Plants! She had totally forgotten about her succulents.

It would give Judith access to her apartment, but it was a risk she'd have to take. She couldn't just leave her apartment for two weeks with no plan for those guys. What if this was the one time of year they needed water and they died because she wasn't there to give it to them? Could she live with herself if she became a plant murderer? She had to ignore the tiny thought that flitted through her brain reminding her that her plants did, in fact, die slow and brittle deaths regularly. It was the intent that mattered. She couldn't intentionally, knowingly, premeditatedly, neglect her plants. It was the difference between murder and manslaughter. And she couldn't go down for that.

"Thanks, Judith, you could check in on my plants, I guess? They shouldn't need much water—just once should cover it."

"You've got it! I won't let you down. I'll clean up a bit while I'm there, too. That's on the house." Judith laughed at her own joke. Reese suppressed a groan. "Now go get on your flight and make your dreams come true!"

Reese clicked off the call. Judith was one-hundred-percent going to hem her pants. Maybe two weeks away from Judith would be like a vacation, even if it had the potential to turn into a Jurassic Park situation. Everything's an adventure until the laws of society break down and then it's a survival story.

FIVE HOURS LATER, she approached the dead silent conference room, just a table of business casual zombies scrolling through their phones. The icy breeze of the air conditioning stung her skin. It was cold enough that she wondered if one of the floor-to-ceiling windows lining the far wall was missing its glass.

Her pulse pounded in her ears. It was like she was wearing her big headphones with no music on. Heartbeat white noise. Reese watched her own traitor hand reach out and knock on the open door. It was a move straight out of an after school special. What was wrong with her? At least she hadn't said 'knock, knock.' There would have been no coming back from that. Get it together, babe.

Ten bodies swiveled in their seats in unison to look at her, she expected them to creak like a creepy animatronic band at a now defunct pizza parlor but someone must have oiled them recently.

"Hello, Ms. Walker." A sultry voice with an undertone greeted her. Either harmless or lethal. She felt a thrill run down her spine.

"Hi, um, Reese is fine." Well, she should just turn around and go back to Detroit now. No one was going to give a speaking job to someone saying um, she might as well have walked in snapping her gum.

The woman who had spoken sat at one end of the oval table. Her glasses were giving off a very hot retro librarian vibe. She was the kind of beautiful that romcoms were always ruining with a makeover. The dark eyes behind the frames stared back at her like the lenses were the only thing keeping them from lasering her to ash.

Reese's mouth was so dry she had to suppress a cough. Had this woman actually lit her on fire and now she had lungs full of smoke? Heat blazed on her face.

A motion next to the stunning woman caught Reese's eye, breaking her trance. David gave her a royal wave then put up his hand. How badly would he embarrass her? He could definitely trust her to check the public humiliation box on her own. David discreetly pushed his mouth closed with his index finger as he nodded in her direction. Reese snapped her mouth shut and gave him a grateful smile. Thank God that's all it was, no childhood nicknames to make this situation worse.

"Glad you could join us, Reese."

"Totally."

The way she said Reese's name sent a current through her that was somewhere between anxiety and arousal. It burned down her spine like a sparkler. Reese was in trouble, and she kind of liked it.

"If you're ready we're all desperate to be freed from the suspense we've been in all day. Why don't you have a seat so we can get started?" The woman gestured to an open chair, her mouth a line as straight and unforgiving as the horizon.

David's expression was carefully blank, but his eyes glimmered as he caught Reese's gaze again. The small smile he sent her way gave her the will to walk to an empty seat instead of bolting.

She'd already lost this job, that was a given. Between the 'um' and arriving a full two hours late. Why not go for broke? She'd just be herself, leave it all out on the table. She dropped her bag next to her chair with a loud thud. "I take it you're Ms. Abbott? Thanks for waiting."

The woman nodded. "Arden."

Reese took her time settling into her chair, crossing her legs and pulling her tablet slowly from her bag. The confidence bluff took her full concentration, and her fingers gripped the glass screen so hard she thought it might shatter. If she was going to get detention, she wanted to really earn it.

Arden's eyes were all over her. She felt them trail over her hands as she unlocked the screen. On her mouth as she quietly cleared her throat. Arden's gaze blazed along her collar bone as she reached up to adjust her necklace. It was already perfectly adjusted, so she just twirled the charm and let the warm petal fall against her skin. Her pale skin flushed beneath Arden's gaze, and she knew anyone looking could follow the progress of her embarrassment like a match dropped in a line of gasoline. A bright and terrible path.

She was thrown off balance and not entirely in a bad way. It was that moment of going into a headstand and holding it beautifully before crashing down and pulling six muscles you didn't know you even had. There was some sort of weird energy in the room. Reese cleared her throat again—it was lined with sandpaper. No way she was going to be able to read without a gallon of water.

"Let me get you some water!" David said right on cue. He hopped up. Gratitude swelled in her chest.

"No, I've got it," Arden said.

Reese turned back and shot her hand out on instinct just in time to catch the bottle of water Arden had slid across the table with the smooth air of a bartender shooting a drink down the bar. All those years of air hockey with Lo in college were finally paying off—one of the few things from her undergrad experience that actually did.

Arden's eyes narrowed as she crossed her arms over her chest. Her dress shirt strained a bit and Reese caught a glimpse of a dark bra beneath the white fabric. Why had she noticed that? She was a professional, and she needed to act like one. Even if the woman sitting across from her seemed to catch all the light in the room, leaving everyone else in shadow. Arden's wavy hair shone with auburn high- lights even in the tremor of fluorescent lights. It was deeply unfair. Reese had taken enough bathroom selfies to know how these industrial lights gave her red hair a tang glow.

Reese took a gulp of water and felt some dribble down

her chin. She was doing the opposite of whatever nailing it was. *Failing it. Even that pun is impossibly bad.* She needed to focus. Surely no one had noticed her self-inflicted waterfall, she'd just ignore it. She definitely wouldn't call attention to it by wiping her mouth or placing her hand over the wet spot on her shirt and pledging allegiance to being eternally awkward. Both of which she was absolutely *not* doing at this very moment.

When she looked up, Arden was still watching her. She felt like a creep, and worse still, an obvious one. When was the last time someone looked at her like that? With focus and enough care to seem truly disappointed. Arden's eyes tracked the final drop of water as it made its way beneath the collar of her shirt.

"Shall we?" Arden said, with a smile that hovered between exasperated and amused—the kind you'd give a toddler having a meltdown in a place that kind of deserved it. Like the DMV or family Christmas.

"Oh, right, sure, let's read some words. I mean, I will. Because that's what you brought me here for." Reese forced a laugh to cover her cringe. Who was this person talking and how had they taken over her brain? Had Judith Freaky Friday-ed her? For the rest of the day she would not say any of her own words if she could help it, because her mouth and brain were two live wires short-circuiting as they fell into the choppy waves of her attraction.

Reese flipped open the folder in front of her and saw a neat stack of manuscript pages, marked with little post-it flags like very important legal documents. A little intense for a kissing book. There was something about the precision of it all, the meticulous sequence of flags on the page, perfectly aligned. Reese could imagine Arden bent over the table placing each note herself. Taking a black marker to neatly obscure the parts she didn't want read.

"Please start with the top scene and read only the portion marked. Whenever you're ready." Arden folded her hands in front of her on the table. She had very nice hands, long fingers and short nails painted a purple so deep it was nearly black. Reese reached for her water.

The serrated cap of the water bottle grated her hand as she twisted it open again to take another ill-advised drink. She hadn't realized people were still paying to drink water from plastic bottles when glasses existed, but ok. She raised the bottle to her mouth as her eyes fell to the opening lines of the scene. She'd use all the free seconds she could steal to prepare.

She'd never read completely cold like this. She liked to do her fire escape practice and really sink her teeth into the scenes, trying out different tones and deliveries. The first line had the main character securing a harness. Reese almost spit out her water but saved it by gracefully choking instead. She felt the warmth course through her body. Ok then. At least part of her was feeling ready.

"You ok?" David half stood from his chair leaning toward Reese.

"Yup," Reese coughed. "Wrong pipe."

"Good thing you didn't follow your dad into plumbing," David said as he sat back down.

Reese narrowed her eyes but didn't reply, her internal groan spoke volumes.

"So, should I just get right into this?" Reese's hands were doing a weird crossing guard motion in front of her that she was powerless to stop. "No preamble to discuss the job?"

"Let's see if those details are necessary after the audition."

"Of course, you want to make sure I can read first," Reese said. She sent a smile across the table that she hoped fell somewhere between self-deprecating and endearing.

From the stern look on Arden's face she gathered it was neither.

And so she began reading:

I threw Sarah on the bed and pushed her knees apart roughly—that was part of our game: the roughness. So was my impatience as I tore at her clothes, leaving a slight snag of desire on the skirt I pulled from her body and tossed over my shoulder. It made a soft snapping sound like a flag in the wind as it fell to the floor.

Reese glanced up just in time to watch David's mouth fall open wide enough to flash his molars. He looked between Reese and Arden with kid-on-Christmas-morning delight sparkling in his eyes. His anticipation took on a life of its own, and Reese watched in horror as he did a little clap before tucking his legs under himself in his chair.

Arden shot him a glare, and Reese wanted to gloat. She couldn't blame him, really. There was something charged and crackling in the air. When she read, Arden's eyes locked on her, and things felt a lot less like fiction and a lot more like foreplay.

The heat between her own legs was a harbinger of distraction, and she was only a few lines in.

"Care to continue?" Arden asked smoothly. Was she not affected?

Reese nodded. She was very fucked. Or very not fucked. Whichever the bad one turned out to be in this scenario.

Arden continued to stare at her in all her beautiful, cold

glory, and Reese felt like the aforementioned skirt, about to be ripped apart and thrown to the floor. It should be unnerving, but with the scene she was reading it had blurred into something strangely erotic. Reese felt electric with the tension in the room. When she touched the table to flip the page, she expected a shock, but all she got was the light sting of a paper cut.

"Of course," Reese said nodding and took a quick sip of water. "I just usually start with an earlier scene."

"This scene is early in the book. It's chapter two."

"Ah," Reese said, trying to keep her face blank even as she could feel her heart beating in her chest.

'ON YOUR KNEES.' *Sarah complied, flipping over with the skill of an Olympic gymnast doing a floor routine. Desire shot through me and I knew I'd need to focus to hold out. Tonight wasn't about me, it was about Sarah and unwinding her bit by bit. About bending her to my will as I bent to hers. I—'*

"THE WAY YOU'RE SAYING 'SARAH' isn't right."

Reese felt hazy as she looked up from the page to the brown eyes boring into her. The tone of the text was impacting her more than usual. She felt powerful and sexy with the ping of excitement she sometimes felt when her favorite song came on. She felt the urgency of the scene in every part of her. She felt on top and ready to top.

Reese wished she hadn't hastily sat so far away from Arden so she could figure out what the fuck was happening right now. Was her breath hitching? Was her heart a snare drum in her chest? Had Reese been a narrating exhibitionist this whole time and just never known it? The last time she read in front of a group was English class, and British lit was definitely more dreary than sexy.

But Judith seemed to get a kick out of listening to her narrate. No, that was practice. This was professional. Neither were personal.

So, was this elaborate professional foreplay? Or was this a totally normal audition and she just needed to get out more? Arden's face gave nothing away. It had been a very long week, and it was only Tuesday afternoon. The sooner she could finish this reading and get out of here and calm down the better.

"Sorry. What did you say?"

Arden sighed. "You're leaving off the h in Sarah. That's not how I imagine it being said." Her speech was slow and deliberate.

"What do you mean imagine? It's a common name."

"More emphasis on the h, the last syllable is 'rah,'" Arden said with a neutral expression as though she wasn't being completely absurd.

This was a test. Or some weird power play. Had this woman never heard anyone say the name Sarah before? She tried to remember all the reasons she should still want this job. Number one, her life would implode without this money.

Reese caught David's eye, and he shot her an I-told-you-so shrug. She took a deep breath, and even though it went against everything she believed as a professional narrator, she readied herself to mispronounce Sarah, one of the most classic names in history, for the remainder of the meeting. There was apparently no pride she wasn't willing to let go of to get this job, and she wasn't sure she liked this new information about herself.

Reese started the scene over, trying to get deeper into the character. God, this was fucking weird. She'd never in her life been watched by an author while reading an intimate scene they'd written. Reading sex scenes seemed like a private act, which was counterintuitive because she did ultimately read them for other people to listen to. Maybe she was being too uptight. Usually if she got turned on it was in the privacy of her own home. But this felt like phone sex through a tin can and a string. And uncomfortable proximity. Or fucking someone while reciting their poems. Way too intimate with a glinting edge of narcissism.

When she glanced up, Arden's eyes were on her mouth. Focusing on the language, most likely. And ways to pull it apart. Her pupils were dilated, turning her already dark eyes to midnight. She was breathing in a way that made her chest move, if this were a novel Reese would call it heaving. Reese felt her heartbeat respond like it was breaking down a locked door.

She's not interested in you—she just likes her own story. Which should be a little bit of a turn off, actually.

The story was getting to Reese, too. Good writing. Plain and simple. This rush of heat to her core was a sign of her professionalism and dedication to her craft. Narrating audiobooks wasn't just reading words on a page. It was acting—embodying the characters. And Reese was going full method.

If Arden was that into Reese's reading, even if what she liked was her own scene, maybe she had a shot at getting this job after all. There had to be some kind of bonus for turning the author on, right? The writing *was* arousing. Objectively. In her professional opinion. Looking at Arden with her intense stare made Reese more aware of the own excitement ticking away low in her stomach.

Arden shifted in her chair. The light caught something silver nestled inside the collar of her shirt and it flashed like a searchlight.

Had the top buttons on Arden's blouse been open this entire time? The glimpse of her neck where it sloped into her shoulder made Reese reach for her water, only to find it already empty. Cool. Cool cool cool.

Arden flipped her dark wavy hair to one side—it was sexy and disheveled, and Reese had a flash of how she must look in the heat of the moment or first thing in the morning after a long night.

A sharp pain in Reese's knee drew her attention. She caught David as he was righting himself in his chair looking smug.

Focus Reesy, you're in it for the money and that's it. This is a job. A weird fucking job, not a weird job fucking. She snapped her eyes back to the page and continued her task.

She was getting close to the end of the first scene, and Sarah's orgasm hovered just beyond the horizon. Reese found she didn't have to fake the breathy quality to her voice as the momentum on the page continued to build. Seeing Arden's face glowing and her hair messy had done something to her. The pulse of excitement between her legs made her feel like poor Sarah—struggling to concentrate until she was allowed to reach the end.

She neared the end of the page just as Sarah was reaching her peak and flipped to the next sheet tearing it a bit in the process. Reese felt like she was the one who needed release. Unprofessional? Or just too good at her craft? Who's to say.

There was some sort of powerful witchcraft happening in this room, and she was powerless against it. She went to continue, ready to see this scene through, but the page in front of her was blank. Reese flipped the page again and saw the beginning of a new chapter that absolutely did not start with a satisfying release.

She released a deep breath. It was Sa-rah's orgasm being denied, not hers, right? Right. But God damn if she wasn't frustrated, she hated leaving a scene unfinished.

"Ok, I think I've heard enough." Arden raked a hand through her chestnut hair and crossed her arms in a way that pushed her cleavage together. A very professional thing to notice.

"Really? I usually read at least three scenes to show range. I'm happy to read the others you have marked here." Reese tapped the pile of papers in front of her.

"I don't think that's necessary. Besides most of us have been in this room too long already." Arden looked at her blankly, like she hadn't just been eye fucking her for the past five pages. She looked calm and collected, her hair now falling neatly at her shoulders. Had she brushed it? Or had Reese imagined the whole thing? She felt like the road-runner realizing suddenly that the cliff had ended and beneath her was just sky.

Arden was right about one thing. She had been in this room long enough. She'd been up since four and was probably delirious with lack of sleep.

"Ok. Thanks for the opportunity, I'll just leave my card." Reese fished a business card from her bag, the matte black cardstock smooth beneath her fingers. Here in this Brooklyn conference room her cards looked a little outdated. She resisted the urge to shove it back in its case. Reese leaned forward to hand her card to Arden, but she made no move to take it. She was focused on the tablet in front of her taking notes.

Reese was stuck in that awkward place, like holding a

door for the person behind you only to realize they are further back than you thought and walking with the slow precision of a person with their shoelaces tied together.

At last, sweet David took pity on her and jumped up to take the card. "Thanks again, Reese. That was great! I mean, whew," he said, fanning himself. "You're staying at the Beaumont on Royal, right?"

"Yeah, I'll be there for tonight at least."

"Great, I'll stop by later and we can get dinner."

She loved David but did not want that at all. Tonight she needed a private hotel room and miles of silence. She'd be willing to compromise and talk to him on the phone for three minutes. Reese started to object, wanting to protect her solitary evening—the only reward at the end of this hellish day, but the hurt that flashed across his face stopped her. It was so much easier to let people down when you weren't looking at them.

"Ok then, see you tonight," Reese said trying to force a smile. She gathered the pages back into the folder and went to slide it into her bag.

Arden's head shot up.

"Leave the folder."

"Right, ok."

"We'll be in touch."

Arden's eyes were back on her iPad before Reese had left the room.

THREE

The boots had been a bad choice. They nipped at Reese's heels as she walked up and down the same block of identical brownstones for either the second or eleventh time. Finding the Beaumont Hotel was looking for Where's Waldo at a candy cane factory—flashes of possibility everywhere, but just another empty decoration. Finally, the small sign propped up in a bay window appeared in the first place she'd looked.

The hotel was in the midst of a mid-century crisis with the blood-red gothic hallway leading jaggedly to her modern room. She shifted the weight of her duffle bag to her other arm and inserted the key card into the hotel room door as her phone rang.

Probably some poor assistant tasked with letting her know she didn't get the job and was booked on the first plane back to Chicago tomorrow morning. Good. She couldn't wait to be out of the disaster city where men tried to touch her arm and give her directions. She was ready to be home.

"This is Reese."

"We've got to work on your intros, babe. Unless you're trying to be an awkward robot. Between your Siri phone voice and knocking on that open conference room door earlier, it's been a tough day for you and first impressions," David said, with a laugh.

"You're hilarious. Good thing this isn't a first impression. So... this call is just to tell me I made a fool of myself today?"

"Only at first, the rest of the reading was hot, and I say that as an objective professional. I'm in no way into the story. The vibe in the room was like going to the club and dancing with a sweaty, sexy, shirtless stranger."

"Gross."

David laughed. "Don't yuck my yum. So, what are you up to?"

"Not much, I just got to my hotel." Reese flipped open her bag and fished out the cord for her headphones. She wanted to make sure they had a full charge so she could block out as much of the classic New York street noise outside her window as possible. Seeing the red charging light illuminate soothed her. Thank God she only had to get through one night in New York.

"You left here like two hours ago. I know city traffic is bad, but your hotel is 20 blocks away—you could have walked it in less time."

"I did walk. Confidently and in the wrong direction for longer than I'll admit before finally consulting a map." Reese stepped to the window and drew the curtains closed; the metallic slide of the rings on the curtain rod was a nice accompaniment to the eclipse of all visible light. The darkness was immediate and lovely. She took her first full, deep breath since she'd left her apartment. If only she could end this call and put on some white noise. She pulled the phone from her ear and swiped up on the screen browsing her silence playlist.

"Why didn't you ask for directions?"

His questions were relentless. But the sooner she answered them, the sooner she could get off the call and soak up some quiet before they met for dinner.

"Asking for directions is a sign of weakness. And then I would've had to talk to some stranger."

"Sure, stranger danger and all that. So, listen, I think I can meet you in an hour or so for dinner. Does that work?"

"Ok."

"Thanks for humoring me with this dinner. I know you probably want to put on your headphones and block out the world."

"What can I say? I'm a sucker for you, Davey. See you soon."

WATER SLUICED over the sides of the tub and settled into tiny ponds on the floor as Reese lowered herself into the bath. The clawfoot tub had been a welcomed surprise in this otherwise tiny hotel room. Like most things boutique and Brooklyn, the room was high on personality and low on practicality. The water burnt her skin like the sun on the first summery day of the year. It was glorious. Tension rose from her muscles like midday heat on a highway, glimmering into nothingness as it merged with the sky.

She slid down and let the water envelop her as she thought about her embarrassing performance. Every weird betrayal her body made in that room, her racing heart and shaky breaths, slammed back into her until she felt like a boat cut loose in a storm. She was out of practice with people, which is why she never should have left her apartment. And it was all for nothing. "We'll be in touch" is the professional brush off. It's the give-me-your-number-I'll-call-you at the end of a night out rather than the mutual confirmation text. At least that's how it worked when she used to go out. Maybe only old people texted now.

She rose back out of the water and dropped her arm over the side of the bath to grab her phone.

"Hey, thanks for calling me back." Lo's voice sounded sleepy.

She always went to sleep early at rehab—the morning yoga session she loved started before dawn.

"I didn't realize I'd missed a call from you."

"Maybe you didn't. I was just assuming because you never call me."

"That's not fair I—well, I text. And besides, haven't we, as a society, moved past the need for audio calls? There are many other forms of communication now—photos, emoji, gifs, those little videos that disappear." Her defense sounded flimsy, even to her. Was she emotionally prepared to back emoji? Maybe Lo was wrong. Reese lowered her phone to check her call log. The last time she'd called Lo was probably a month ago. Definitely no more than six. Completely respectable.

"Reese." Lo's voice had a sharp edge that told her she'd missed something.

"Hmm?" She tucked the phone back between her ear and shoulder. She could check her call history later and text Lo a screenshot of it.

There had to be more important ways to care for people than calling them and *telling* them you care. She sent her a sparkle heart emoji at least once a day. If that wasn't love, nothing was.

"I asked if you were really going to advocate for print media when you record audiobooks for a living."

"Maybe I never call because my voice is tired and I have to protect it."

"It's not too late to get your voice insured."

"No, it's too early." Reese ran her free hand through the water.

"Where are you—it sounds all echoey?"

"I'm in the bath."

"If we didn't have a history of bathing together as kids I might find it weirder that you're calling me while indisposed. But I've seen your ass and I can never unsee it, so this is nothing."

"That's sweet, Lo. Glad to see all that therapy is cracking open your sensitive side."

Lo's laugh was a low rumble Reese felt in her chest and it made her long to be home. Being so far away felt deeply wrong, like a simmering memory that you'd left the stove on.

"So, you got a bathtub installed at your apartment? Any other life-shattering changes you'd like to tell me about, Reesy? Do you have a new blender, too?"

"I could have been more clear, I'm in a bathtub in New York. I came here for a job audition that I totally messed up."

"Wait, what?"

"Yeah, unexpected, right? This hotel is boutique, which means tiny but with unexpected amenities. There's a seltzer machine in the hall."

"That's not the part of your sentence I was reacting to. And I think you know that."

"Fine, fine. I meant to call you before I left, but it all happened so fast." Reese sank down in the tub and the warm water lapped against her shoulders. It was strange to be in this different place that wasn't her apartment, and unsettling to feel almost ok there. But she also felt less substantial somehow, like she was diluted. The water continued to wash over her, each wave a bit more relaxing than the last. She imagined she was a sandcastle melting in the waves.

She realized Lo was still talking and sloshed around a bit to sit up and listen.

"Happened so fast, as in, they sent a helicopter and kidnapped you while you were sleeping? This is huge! How could you not tell me?"

"Because I was nervous, and I was right to be! I totally messed up my chance today. I was really late and the author hated me I think. Well, she seemed into it while I was reading but then ended the audition after a few minutes and told me they'd be in touch." A memory of Arden watching her read like she was the only person in the room flashed through her head. She replayed Arden sinking her teeth into her lower lip in concentration and something low in her stomach clenched in response.

"Isn't her telling you they'd be in touch a *good* thing? You can't just make things bad because you want them to be."

"Want to bet? And no, it's like ending a date by saying I'll call you. Have you ever once called?"

"Yes, of course, I've called. Have you never called after saying that? What's wrong with you? Why say it at all?"

"You say it to end the date. It's a figure of speech like 'I had a great time' or 'this was fun.'"

"So what are you going to do if you get this job and have to stay and actually interact with Arden Abbott every day?"

"Can you stop saying her name like some sort of celebrity? I'm not even going to worry about that. I'll be back in my apartment by lunchtime tomorrow recording in my closet." But until then she'd enjoy the warm water in the humongous tub and as soon as she got off of this call, she'd enjoy a little peace and quiet, too. It was good to have goals.

"We'll see about that. You don't give yourself enough credit. I bet she liked you more than you think."

A loud knock at the door made Reese jump, spilling more water onto the floor.

"Shit, Lo, I've gotta go. David is meeting me for dinner, and he just got here."

"Why were you taking a bath when you had dinner plans?"

"Can we do this later? I was trying to relax enough to get through dinner. Let's talk later. Love you."

"Love you too! Give Davey a kiss for me and tell him to come to visit his favorite Walker sister."

"I just told you," Reese smirked, "we're visiting right now. I'll call you tomorrow, Lolo. Love you."

THE SILK ROBE was sticking to her damp skin in a way that was a little obscene. David wouldn't mind. They'd spent summers skinny dipping in Lake Huron, the icy waves taking away their breath and inhibitions. Though, now that she thought about it, she mostly went in the water to make sure Lo was safe—the story of her life. She would have been happy on the beach, sifting cool sand beneath her feet and searching the stars for constellations she'd read about.

Reese reached for the door handle without bothering to check the viewfinder. Something she never would have done at home, but Judith was 1,000 miles away. No one could bother her here. She could already picture the shock on David's face and the way it would fade into laughter as he took in her skimpy robe and disheveled state.

She threw open the door like a teenager being paid $7 an hour to haunt people on the weekends. The face on the other side of the door was definitely stunned, but it wasn't David's.

Arden Abbott stood in the hotel hallway, her mouth slightly open in surprise, looking like some goddess. Her hair was gathered up in a high bun and a few dark strands had escaped to trail down her neck. She was holding her jacket by her side like she's maybe been there a while or planned to stay.

Reese's own yelp echoed through her ears followed by the bang of the hotel room door as she slammed it shut. She slumped back against it as she worked to steady her breaths. What the hell was Arden Abbott doing at her hotel? Was that a normal thing—people just showing up places? And what had she been thinking just opening a door like that? It could have been anyone—a concierge, a murderer, a mailman with more bad news. Any of those would have been better than this terrible, beautiful woman. This terrible, beautiful woman who had now seen Reese in basically nothing. She looked down at the robe, had it shrunk since she put it on? Maybe if she wished hard enough she could teleport back to two days ago in her apartment.

"Reese, is everything ok? Do you think you could open the door?" Arden sounded unsure, stopping just short of soothing.

But Reese startled anyway. What kind of monster waits patiently after they get a door slammed in their face? Reese let the silence stretch between them. Arden could sit with her uncertainty while Reese figured out the best way to escape a third story hotel room.

"Reese. Are you ok in there? I need to talk to you about the book." Arden's tone had an edge, like she used the silence as a whetstone to sharpen it.

She'd just seen everything Reese had to offer, and she wanted to know if she was *ok*? Nothing about this day had been ok. But Reese did need to talk about the job because for some cruel reason all of her problems had not magically disappeared since yesterday. A shot at recording this book was the entire reason she was in this mess in the first place.

Reese looked down at the silk robe, hoping it wasn't as bad as she thought it was. But it was worse. It was white bikini bad. The wet fabric was clinging to what it was supposed to conceal, revealing the curve of her breasts. It was a strange thing, to be betrayed by a garment. She'd just flashed Arden Abbott. David had really jinxed her with that first impressions comments.

"I'm not decent enough for a business conversation." Reese pressed her ear to the door, resting her cheek on her hand like a lady eavesdropping in a period drama. As embarrassed as she was she also didn't really want her to leave.

"I'm, um... aware," Arden's voice seemed to hitch. "Do you think putting on more clothes would help? Or I could try to even the playing field if you toss me a robe." Her laugh was a low rumble like rolling thunder. Reese loved a storm.

She glanced at the extra robe hanging on the back of the bathroom door. The thought of Arden in it sent a sharp bolt of desire through her.

"Reese, this silence is a little much. Please tell me you're not climbing out the window. I meant it as a joke, not a proposition. Sorry, I feel like I've made this weird."

She'd answered the hotel room door basically naked and

Arden was worried *she* made it weird. Well, something was definitely weird. Reese wasn't used to this strange swirl of desire. She wanted to hold it up to the light and examine it.

"Fine, just give me a minute."

"Take all the time you need." Through the door, Reese could hear Arden's muffled chuckle.

The yoga pants and cutoff t-shirt she'd thrown on were sticking to her still damp skin unpleasantly, but even those thin layers of cotton and spandex felt like a kind of armor as she prepared to face Arden again. Plus, all the yoga she'd been doing at home had made her arms look really good.

Reese glanced at the viewfinder in the door, a perfect circle as dark as a bullethole. Such a simple device that would have saved her a world of trouble. She wondered what she'd see if she looked through it now. Arden had been quiet as Reese put on clothes, quieter than Reese realized she was capable of being. Maybe she'd decided to leave? The thought of Arden leaving sent a strange ping of disappointment through her.

But she'd have to parse that later because when she peered into the hall Arden was still there being stunning and perfect and absolutely way too much to handle. A fresh wave of heat swept through Reese settling low in her stomach. Definitely still warm from the bath and not some combustive reaction to the way Arden was leaning against the far wall with one leg bent like a 50s heartthrob.

Arden's head was tilted down looking at her phone and a few strands of dark hair fell across her face. It was red in places where it caught the hallway light. Reese gave herself a few seconds to take in her perfection, feeling every inch of her own disheveled and flushed appearance.

Finally, her curiosity won out and she opened the door.

Pretend to be confident, most people can't tell the difference. Or most people are pretending and there is no difference.

Reese squared her shoulders and ran the flat of her palm over her stomach to smooth out the wrinkles. Arden's gaze tracked her fingertips. She slipped into her ice queen voice. "So, Ms. Abbott, what brings you to my hotel room at night?"

"It's a little unexpected, I guess," she said with a shrug, "but I was in the neighborhood for a meeting. I thought I'd stop by to talk about your audition earlier."

"Ok." What was there to talk about? Arden had dismissed her before she'd even read a full scene. This time tomorrow Reese would be back in her apartment avoiding Judith.

"You were good. The reading was sexy."

Had she heard that right? Nothing about the way Arden dismissed her earlier made Reese think her reading had been good.

"Oh." Reese's throat went dry as she forced a swallow. What was it with this woman making her completely inarticulate? She talked for a living. Literally. But for the second time today, Arden had left her unable to use words.

Arden shifted on her feet. She watched Reese's face expectantly, but Reese had nothing. "You know," Arden brought a hand to her forehead but it seemed forced like she was trying to fill the silence, "I'm realizing from the way you answered the door before that you were maybe expecting someone else?" Arden's eyes widened as she wound her way through her question. "Maybe I should go?"

Arden made no move to leave.

"No, I don't want you to go." The words were out of Reese's mouth before she could even process them. Reese nodded, grateful for Arden's help to get through this conversation. "I mean," Reese cleared her throat and tried to get the ice back in her voice, "It's ok, really. I was just expecting David."

Arden's brows drew into a knot of confusion as her eyes trailed down Reese's body. She caught herself with a start and jerked her head back up with the violence of someone who had fallen asleep sitting up.

Reese could still feel the heat of Arden's gaze where it had lingered on the expanse of skin along her side. The armholes she'd cut in the shirt sloped down to the bottom of her ribs. She knew if Arden looked hard enough she'd see Reese was braless. Which was a very practical choice, really. Putting on a bra right after a bath was like putting on a straitjacket—she didn't want to get stuck and have to call Arden in for backup. Though with the way Arden was looking at her now, maybe she should have.

"I didn't realize you and David were... close like that."

Reese caught her knee-jerk protest in mid-reflex as she watched the smirk appear on Arden's face. She was teasing her. Reese could deal with teasing.

"What can I say? We've known each other since grade school, he's seen it all." Reese raised her eyebrows but didn't elaborate. It was oddly fun to make Arden squirm a bit, especially with the discomfort of the audition fresh in her mind. Teasing was one of her love languages, and she didn't want to parse out why she was using it with Arden beyond the fact that she looked very cute with her face all scrunched up in confusion like that.

"Right." Arden tilted her head but said nothing. Instead, she shoved her hands into her pockets as she scuffed one of her boots back and forth against the blood-red hallway carpet. For a minute that repetitive whoosh was the only sound between them. Reese found it oddly soothing, like deep ocean white noise—the kind she'd listen to as she drifted off to sleep.

Reese felt her eyes grow heavy and shook her head to break her trance. "So what did you want to talk about from the audition? Do you have some notes for next time?"

"Not notes. I know things were left uncertain at the audition."

"Uncertain?" Reese raised an eyebrow. She usually did anything she could to end a conversation with someone new. "Are you referring to when you dismissed me after reading one scene?"

"Right, that. And your being several hours late." Arden's smile took the sting out of her comment.

Reese drew in a deep breath, her heart fluttered in her throat as she prepared to ask the question that had been haunting her since she left Arden earlier. It might be too late for this job, but at least she could use Arden's feedback to improve for the future. "Was there something wrong with my voice that you didn't like?"

Arden looked down at the ground. It was hard to tell in the dim hallway light if she was blushing or if Reese just wanted her to be. "No. Your voice was perfect. Powerful and sexy. It was... it was perfect." Arden's voice had dropped almost to a whisper by the end of her sentence, and Reese leaned into the hallway to hear her better. When Arden looked up their faces were close enough that Reese could feel the warm brush of Arden's breath on her cheek.

"Oh." Reese didn't pull back. She knew she should but her desire to close the distance between them and to retreat were in a tug-of-war and she was using all of her strength not to find out what Arden's lips tasted like.

Arden took a half step backward putting some space between them. Reese felt a draft cut through the thin t-shirt like a winter wind. She stepped back out of the cold hallway into the safety of her room.

"Anyway, like I was saying," Arden smoothed her hands over her hair and shifted her voice a little deeper, " your audition was solid, and my agent, Sophia, is really anxious to get this project back on track. And I am, too. So, I have a proposal for you."

Arden had rushed the last part out so quickly that it took Reese a second to process it.

"I don't believe in marriage." Why did she say that? Reese felt the cringe down to her toes. Now she's going to think *you're* thinking about marriage. Why was she devoted to making this weirder?

Arden's eyes went wide. "Wh—what?"

"As an institution. I know it can make sense for tax purposes, but I see it as more of a relic that just extends misery." Reese wanted desperately to stop talking but she was incapable of making it happen. *This is serious. Be serious.*

"No, I meant what are you talking about marriage for."

"You're the one who has a proposal, Arden." It had been so long since she had talked to a new person that Reese had forgotten her jokes weren't for everyone.

"Arden."

Now it was Reese's turn to be confused. Conversations were not usually this difficult at least from what she remembered. Though maybe during all those days in her apartment she had blocked out how terrible it was to try to understand another person.

"What?"

"My friends call me Arden"

"Your friends call you by your regular, full name?" Reese said with a laugh. "I think I missed when we became friends. A minute ago, you were proposing. Next we'll be colleagues and then merely acquaintances. I feel like we're regressing."

This energy between her and Arden didn't feel like friendship. Reese wasn't entirely sure what it felt like. This afternoon she thought Arden had rejected her work—rejected her—but tonight she seemed kind, almost normal if a little strange. And she was here, wasn't she? Showing up at Reese's hotel room unannounced seemed... nice, if deeply weird.

Arden paused, seeming to consider the question. "Well, hopefully we'll start with colleagues and either move forward or backward from there." Arden bent down and dug through the bag at her side. She slid a thick sheaf of papers from a folder and handed them to Reese. Most of her contracts were one-page PDFs that she signed with the precision of a kid wielding a purple crayon on a white wall. This had the heft of a great American novel. This was a tome. Once again little multicolored flags poked out from the pages like birthday candles. This woman must have stock in office supplies.

Reese thumbed through the pages and then lowered them to her side. "Thanks, I'll look through these later."

"I don't mind waiting."

"You don't mind waiting while I read this 300-page contract? Does it include your entire book?"

"It's 72 pages, actually. All of them are important." Arden crossed her arms but made no move to leave.

"Ok, so it only includes part of your book? The first five chapters?"

"Why don't you start looking through it and find out? Bring the signed copy with you tomorrow morning. We start at nine am sharp."

"That's a little presumptuous. What makes you think I'm going to say yes?" She was definitely going to say yes. She hadn't come all the way to New York to not jump at the chance to save herself from the collection's agency swooping down for carrion.

"I think you want to see how the story ends." Arden said with a wink. Reese watched her saunter down the hall until she disappeared into the elevator.

What the hell had just happened?

THE STATIC OF the intercom crackled in Reese's headphones and she flinched, already knowing what was coming.

Arden's sweet voice sliced into the middle of yet another sentence Reese was reading.

"I think you could pause for a split second longer on the comma. You're rushing the moment of contemplation."

"It's not even dialogue. What is being contemplated? Whether or not the commas are excessive?" Reese mumbled.

"What's being contemplated is the second half of the sentence."

The worst part of all this professional-grade equipment was that the mics picked up *everything*. Every swallow, every breath, every eye roll. And Arden gleefully caught each one and threw it back against the glass separating them for examination.

Reese gritted her teeth. She tried to keep her tone steady, but it was like an electric sander bucking against the grain of this conversation.

"Ok, I'll try it again with a longer pause, but I think if

you'd just let me read through a full scene, then these things would start to fall into place."

"How about this—let's have a working lunch. You can keep rehearsing, and then depending on how that goes, after lunch we'll try it your way."

"My way as in me narrating this book like I'm being paid to do?"

"Something like that. Now, do you want a smoothie or a salad?"

"I want pizza."

"Smoothies it is. It will be easier for you to practice if you're not trying to chew food. Trust me.

Reese's stomach contracted in protest. She just needed to get through this day. Get some words recorded and really secure this job.

How could anyone sound so nice when being such a complete pain in the ass?

If the morning felt like learning to drive a stick shift where Reese stalled out with each mid-sentence correction from Arden, lunch rehearsal over smoothies was the inevitable crash into a tree.

Arden dragged a stool into the studio space, its legs screeching across the floor. The noise was the kind of horrible that David could use as a sound effect for a slasher audiobook. The shrill note sent a chill down Reese's spine, but Arden didn't even flinch. She pulled the seat directly in front of Reese, so close that their knees brushed when Arden crossed her legs. And Reese felt the heat of her everywhere.

Why was she so close? The room smelled warm and sweet like vanilla and nutmeg. Reese felt like she was standing in front of an open oven with Arden so close, the heat wafting off the cookies baking inside. This space was not meant for two people. It was barely meant for one. She couldn't avoid Arden's gaze.

Arden squinted at Reese. She opened her mouth then closed it again without saying anything. Reese tried to keep her face neutral. The sooner Arden started talking the sooner this would end, right? Inside, the winds of her panic were picking up speed. Or at least that's what she thought it was. She tried to dig up her feelings from the last time she had a panic attack a few years ago. Like flipping through a terrible yearbook. Here's the first time Lauren went to rehab and called Reese's driving her there unforgivable. Here's the time her girlfriend did drugs in front of Lo. Here's her leaving you when Reese got upset about it. Reese closed the book. There was a reason she kept her world contained these days—no nasty surprises for her to stumble through.

"I was thinking you could read the first chapter and I'll give you notes. That way after lunch we can make some actual progress."

The only thing keeping them from making actual progress were Arden's notes and helpful tips. Reese took a deep breath to block the frustrated words she could feel clawing their way up. Her best bet was to hurry this along. Get this day over and start again tomorrow once she'd had an uninterrupted evening to calm down. She thought of closing the shades in her hotel and turning her phone off; completely unreachable like floating in an isolation chamber. The rhythm of her heart stuttered and smoothed a bit at the thought, like a needle catching the groove in a favorite record.

And then Arden tapped her pen loudly on the table and Reese pictured her peaceful night interrupted by Arden, barreling through her hotel room door like the Kool Aid man. Though once she'd gotten past the shock of it she realized she hadn't necessarily hated Arden showing up and changing the course of her night, her week, her month. But where was that Arden now? The one who had told Reese her voice was perfect?

Arden bit down on the end of her pen while she scanned her notes. Reese couldn't look anywhere but her mouth, her bottom lip pouting slightly as she twirled her pen. Her lip gloss was barely there, just enough to make her lips shimmer slightly, not a color, just a highlight of her perfect—

"Reese, can you pay attention? We have a lot of notes to get through here." Arden glanced down at the notebook in front of her, a bulleted list of Reese's failures both real and imagined. Reese could have saved her the trouble and shared her working copy.

Reese's jaw was a vise as she nodded. She closed the door on her thoughts of last night. Arden was now frowning a bit, which made her mouth a lot less distracting at least. Mind over matter.

She could do twenty minutes. Arden had notes on every sentence, and the constant interruptions kept Reese from hitting any kind of rhythm. She could hear the choppiness in her narration. Her sentences interrupted by the constant speed bumps of helpful corrections. For the first time since she could remember, Reese felt truly bad at reading. She kept waiting for Arden to yank her out of the recording booth with one of those long vaudeville canes.

She dug her fingers into the sides of her cup until they went numb and frost white from her cold drink. And how the hell had they gone with smoothies. They've been working for hours and somehow berries and some water were supposed to give her the will to keep going?

Reese was unable to hit any kind of rhythm. Which led

to more notes from Arden. For the first time since second grade, she had mispronounced the word 'pronunciation,' putting an 'o' where it shouldn't be, and the irony was not lost on her. She couldn't do this.

Her ears filled with rushing wind.

"Reese!"

Reese blinked, clearing her vision enough to see Arden snapping her fingers.

Reese's fingers itched to swat Arden's hand down.

"The sooner we get this done, the sooner we can get back to work." Arden lowered her hand to her lap.

Waves of frustration crashed into the breaker wall of her resolve. Sweat prickled on the back of her neck like drops of sea spray flinging themselves over the edge. Reese swayed in her chair. Through the edges of her darkening vision, she saw concern flash across Arden's face.

"Just a few more minutes of practice, ok? Then we can get back to work." Arden's voice was almost a whisper.

The rush in Reese's ears picked it up and scattered her words.

Reese couldn't take a few more minutes. She had to leave this room right now or she'd drown. Her lungs felt waterlogged, and she couldn't get the air she needed. She wanted to throw her smoothie against the glass and watch it streak down horribly.

But if she was going to lose her composure, she would not be doing it in this fucking studio over smoothies. And if she needed to throw something or slip under the waves of panic for a bit, it would not be here because she still needed this job. Lo needed rehab. That's what she needed to focus on, making sure her sister was ok.

Thinking of Lo made an anchor drop in her chest dragging her down a little more. She was failing everyone. She had to get herself out of this room before the panic wrapped around her ankles and pulled her under completely.

Her hand was on the door before she fully registered that she was leaving.

"Ok, you're right, let's take a five min—"

The soundproof door of the studio swung shut behind Reese, sealing Arden inside with her cheerful words.

Outside the cold wind caught the edges of her leather jacket and whipped behind her like a sail carrying her away. The sharp scent of coming snow was painful and grounding as she breathed it in. She crossed the street and started to walk.

FOUR

The studio was bathed in darkness. The glowing screen of Arden's phone lit up her face from below, casting an eerie ghost story glow.

Reese eased the door open, trying to go undetected. Arden wasn't wearing headphones. How did people go through life like that? Just absolutely drowning in the cacophony of daily life like it was somehow pleasant and unobtrusive? Reese hesitated. Maybe she could just leave her stuff overnight—how badly did she need a phone, wallet, and hotel key card? She thought about trying to explain her situation to the concierge with no form of ID. The guaranteed labyrinth of that conversation was enough of a push for her to open the door fully.

Reese took a few steps into the room. She'd do her best to smooth it over. Arden had ruined her day, but she could be cool about it. "So, it takes real talent, but it turns out you can get lost in New York, even on the grid system."

"You got lost? David said you'd come back, but I was starting to doubt it."

"Nah, I always come back. David and I go way back, so

he's a reliable source. Unless he tells you that I cheat at games, in which case he's a sore loser. And he's lying. Speaking of David..." Reese looked around the studio, but David had not magically materialized to save her from this encounter in the 30 seconds she and Arden had been talking.

Arden gave a faint laugh and threaded her arms into the jacket she'd had resting across her lap. Had she been waiting for Reese to get back before she left? "He had dinner plans to get to. The sun went down almost an hour ago."

"To be fair, the sun goes down at noon on the East Coast in winter, so that's not a reliable measure of time. As a society, we've moved past using the sun to tell time."

"And what were *you* using as a reliable measure of time? Since it wasn't the sun or your phone, which I called only to hear it ring right near me."

"How cold and tired I felt. I knew I'd gone too far when my hands went numb."

"Well, go warm up, I guess. I'm glad you're ok. Have a good night."

Arden passed close to her in the tight space of the studio to get to the door. Another wave of vanilla and nutmeg hit Reese and with it came an unfamiliar urge to make up for disappearing. Panic attacks were hard to understand and even harder to explain. It was easier to let them come across as flakiness, but she couldn't do that here.

The day had been a total waste, and some of that was even Reese's fault. What if she woke up tomorrow and didn't have a job? She was already two days closer to Lo's rehab bill being sent to collections, and she was also down $11 for a smoothie that was sitting in a puddle of its own making on the table in front of her.

She hadn't needed to track money so closely in years, but it was hard for her to breathe under the weight of this overdue bill. Everything was reminding her of the worst parts of her childhood today. All of those times she tried her best to make ends meet and still fell short. Back then she threw herself into books to escape, and now, she kind of still did that, but called it work. At least that would give her something to anchor onto so she could pull herself out of this tailspin.

"Hey Arden?"

Arden paused, her hand on the door. When she turned to Reese her face looked more concerned than truly angry. Reese felt a flash of hope in her chest.

"Yeah?"

"How long were you going to wait here for me to come back?"

"As long as it took to make sure you were ok, I guess." Arden shrugged and dropped her gaze to the floor. She seemed almost nervous with her admission.

"Oh." Reese was dredging the depths of her mind for more words, but all she was catching was a bunch of useless debris. She still couldn't make sense of Arden. Most people were so predictable, they stayed on one track, but Arden kept jumping the curb and crashing into the stands. It was exciting and chaotic and a little dangerous. Reese had no issue dealing with people she found annoying, she just literally shut them out and locked the door. But the ones who intrigued her wrecked her carefully orchestrated life.

"Ok, I'll leave you to it then." Arden didn't move to leave.

Reese saw the metaphor of it—how Arden had opened the door and now she stood in the liminal space between continuing this day and ending it, once again waiting on Reese.

"Wait. I'm feeling better now. If you don't have somewhere to be, do you want to see if we can get a chapter recorded? I mean, you probably have plans, though."

"Nothing I can't miss. And it would be nice to tell my agent we made some progress today. But do you know how to use all the equipment? Because I have no idea what I'm doing. The most technical I get is opening a new word doc."

"How hard can it be? I record on my computer from home all the time."

It was hard. Reese spent twenty minutes deciphering the various buttons and knobs of the soundboard, and even then, she'd only really figured out the volume, intercom, and, thankfully, how to record.

"So, you just press this button to record." Reese pointed to the button on the sound board while Arden nodded, and, bless her, took notes on her phone. "I'll give you a thumbs up to tell you when, so you don't need to mess with the intercom. That way it doesn't get left on and mess with the audio."

Reese reached for her water glass and found it empty. The two chapters she'd read back-to-back had flown by. Arden had offered no corrections, and she'd hit her stride with the characters, finding their comedic timing and tones at last. She took her first full deep breath since arriving in New York; maybe this project would be ok after all. Reese stood from the uncomfortable stool; her lower back felt like it had gone through a trash compactor. She stretched her arms above her head, feeling the rush of cool air on her stomach as she leaned from side to side. She looked to the window just in time to see Arden jerking her head back down and sliding a lever.

When Reese entered the booth, Arden was in a trance, poking at the sound board until it glowed.

"So, what did you think?"

Arden lowered the headphones gently around her neck delicately, as if they were a string of tropical flowers too precious to crush.

"Much better. I know you hated it at the time, but all the practice from earlier really paid off." Arden shot her a satisfied smile and Reese could see the appeal of making her happy, if it meant even sometimes getting a smile like that in return.

"I'm glad. Should we play it back?" Reese's heart sped up at the thought of sitting next to Arden and listening to the chapters. Would the raw audio be as good as she thought?

"Isn't that bad luck? Shouldn't we wait for David to edit it?" Arden hesitated, her hand hovering over the playback button.

"No, we can listen now. It won't jinx anything."

Reese settled on the seat next to Arden, letting their arms brush and not minding one bit. How much had changed in this one-full-year of a day. A few faint freckles speckled Arden's face like city stars, faintly making their presence known if you cared enough to look. Reese hadn't known to look for them before. And she loved stargazing. In that moment she realized she was absolutely fucked.

Under no circumstances should she be focusing on nice things about this woman. This total perfectionist who had literally given her a panic attack earlier because she didn't like how she said some words. Which, for the record, was perfectly. Just because they'd had one good hour didn't negate the past two days of terror. This was a job she was suffering through.

But still, Reese didn't bother to look for another set of headphones. She lifted the ones from Arden's neck, her fingers ghosting across her soft warm skin as she lifted them over her head. Reese held the headphones between them. When Arden leaned in she held Reese's gaze until their foreheads nearly touched. Reese dug her nails into her palm to physically restrain herself from closing her eyes and the distance between them. *Get it together.*

Reese reached across Arden to hit the button for playback, as her arm brushed Arden's sweater she felt sparks on her skin. *Fantastic.*

When she got back to Chicago, Reese needed to figure out a way to spend more time with people. She was confusing this one ok interaction, inflating it. She absolutely had to shoot it down. This wasn't an attraction, just loneliness masquerading as one.

Reese heard a slight crackle over the speakers, and her heart leapt as she waited for the audio to begin. A minute went by and... nothing happened. She punched the play button again a little more forcefully this time. Still, just a crackling silence that she had to lean in close enough to feel Arden's breath on her face to hear.

Her heart lurched like she'd reached the top of a rollercoaster, that suspended moment where you knew you were about to fall. She wanted to scream in terrible anticipation.

The silence stretched out between them.

"Did you hit record?"

"Of course, I *hit record*. I can follow simple instructions, Reese."

"Ok. And you're sure the lights on the board lit up?"

A noise came over the headphones at last. Arden laughing at something Reese had read. Arden laughing at her own joke.

"You recorded in the booth."

"No, I didn't. You must not have set it up right. I did exactly what you said—you're the expert."

Reese pushed down her frustration at the lost work and wasted time. A momentary solution. She tried to remember that she'd get paid either way. But beneath it, all the fire of her annoyance flashed blue. Putting her faith in someone else had once again been a colossal mistake.

It wasn't just that they'd lost work, but they'd lost her best work so far. The only time in two days where she felt solidly competent. Maybe the only thing that was worth keeping and securing this job for her. Arden's laughter in the recording continued to swarm between them antagonizing Reese. She refused to feel satisfied that her reading had hit the right notes. Of course it did. She was a professional, and she was here to do a job, not make friends or whatever this was with the author.

"I can't believe none of that got recorded."

"Let's just count it as more practice and hope it pays off tomorrow." Arden shrugged, shoved her computer into her bag and headed for the door.

FIVE

A whistle chirped right beside Reese's ear, causing her game driver to crash into a wall in a ball of flames. The one time she wasn't wearing her headphones, she was met with an auditory assault.

"Shit." Reese closed the game and slid her phone into her pocket.

"Good morning to you too, sunshine." David yanked his wool hat off and ran a hand over his closely cropped black hair.

"You let the ghosts win, Davey."

"I wasn't the one driving. I can't believe you still pick the skeleton, he doesn't even have any good clothes."

"That's because *her* superpower is not caring what anyone thinks."

"Fine, she's a deceased role model. I've always found her... humerus." David raised his eyebrows at her. "Want to get set up? Oh, before I forget, I gave Arden your coffee order, hope that was ok."

"I'm not sure if I should be more upset by that terrible skeleton pun or by your complete violation of my privacy."

"Really? Your latte preference is classified?"

"How someone takes their coffee is a very intimate detail, Davey. At least in my world."

"Look, she called and said she was going to stop on her way in. Let her be nice."

"Being nice is a form of manipulation. You see the way she treats me. It's like I can't do anything right. And last night was a total disaster. We never should have tried recording without you."

"I'm sorry, you did what?" David shot his arm out without turning to face her, barring Reese from entering the studio. She stumbled backward and crashed into the wall behind her, which turned out to be Arden leading with a tray of coffees. The spill happened in slow motion like liquid in a lava lamp, but it soaked her all the same.

The coffee hit between Reese's shoulder blades and tracked down the length of her spine. A few mouthfuls made their way intimately down beneath the waist of her jeans. It was not welcomed.

A puddle gathered on the oak floor of the studio and Reese watched as it was slowly absorbed by the carpeting lining the hallway.

The pain of the initial burn was already starting to fade as the air cooled the hot liquid. Reese had to restrain herself from stripping off her clothes immediately. Everything felt ruined.

She pulled her shirt up and held it scrunched in her hand just below her bra. There was an angry red mark curving around her side that disappeared beneath the waist of her black jeans. When she looked up Arden's eyes were hovering on the curve of her hip with a fierce concentration.

"Ok then," Reese shook her hands and watched more droplets of coffee fly off. A few of them hit Arden, and she startled and lifted her head. *Well, that's what you get for checking out the woman you just maimed.*

Arden was dabbing at her own drenched shirt with a single paper napkin that was disintegrating in her hand. She offered it meekly to Reese, and took a step back to avoid contact.

"You should just take your shirt off and wring it out. I'm going to head back to my hotel and get cleaned up—there's no hope for these clothes." Reese plucked at her absolutely trashed dress shirt—the nicest one she'd brought. "Should we meet back here in an hour?"

"No. You can't leave. We have to record." Arden moved to stand between Reese and the exit.

This was unreal. Did this woman care about anything besides work? She was lucky Reese wasn't threatening litigation. She gritted her teeth. "It wasn't a question, Arden. I can absolutely leave. I'm soaked in coffee that *you* spilled on me. I am going to my hotel to shower." She enunciated each word with fierce precision. There was no 'we' in recording. Reese narrated. Arden just... supervised? Interrupted? Was a very distracting, very attractive, completely stunning total pain in the ass?

"Funny because *I'm* soaked in coffee that *you* spilled." Arden's face gave no indication that she was aware of the absurdity of her statement. "But we don't have time to waste today. We need to make real progress that I can show my agent. I need something tangible."

"It's an audiobook. The medium itself is intangible." Screaming was a bad idea. She shouldn't strain her voice so early in the day. She'd have to settle for screaming inside her heart instead. Reese was being pedantic about the tangible thing—she knew what Arden meant. But every ounce of frustration about Arden constantly nitpicking her readings and yesterday's lost audio was bubbling to the surface. The tension boiled in the air between.

Arden closed her eyes. Her mouth drew into a thin line. Reese needed to push while she had her on the ropes.

"I burned my skin, Arden. You did, too. Your agent can relax, just tell her what happened. Or don't tell her anything, and we'll just make up the time later."

Arden mumbled something Reese couldn't hear. Her wet clothes were now cold against her skin and she shuddered. Her patience was as empty as the coffee cups scattered across the studio floor.

"What was that?" Reese fought to keep the exasperation in her voice to a respectable, office-appropriate level. God, she missed working from home, blissfully alone.

"Sophia doesn't relax. She's checking in at noon. There is no later, Reese. I can't believe I messed this up. Even when I'm working so hard to be perfect, I just ruin it anyway. Maybe everyone's right. Maybe I can't be trusted."

Whoa. That seemed extreme. As far as she knew Arden was a successful author. Why would anyone ever doubt her with her track record of best sellers? The tears in Arden's eyes caught the light. Something inside of Reese stopped short. She saw a glimmer in Arden like a piece of broken glass in the sand—something human and imperfect and finally understandable. It was like one of those magic eye posters, where the image reveals itself for just a moment when you catch it just right.

There seemed to be a lot more going on beneath the surface if Arden was so upset. This setback seemed minor, even with her agent checking in. Annoying and inconvenient, but minor through and through.

"You shouldn't cry over spilled milk. Even if it was

mixed with your coffee." Reese's joke was terrible, and she cringed waiting for Arden's reaction.

Arden gave a gurgling laugh. "I think that's the worst joke I've ever heard. It was perfect." She laughed again and swiped at her eyes with the napkin she'd been clutching before recoiling from the coffee-soaked pulp. The move left a bit of mascara streaked beneath her lashes. Reese had always had a weakness for messy eye makeup—the way it screamed morning after and a certain vulnerability. As she continued to watch Arden, the ground beneath them seemed to be shifting, and she wasn't sure she liked it.

Reese needed to leave immediately. She definitely needed some space before she felt anything more for Arden. She'd go back to her hotel. Shower. Remember she wasn't here to make friends. She didn't need any new people in her life, she already had David and Lo.

The intercom crackled, and Arden clutched Reese's arm as they both jumped. Reese took in David's grin. Jesus, had he been there the whole time? The window separating the studio from the controls reminded Reese of the two-way glass in interrogation rooms. When David raised his hand and gave a small wave she desperately wished she couldn't see him and vice versa. His voice came over the speakers like a school principal calling them to the office.

"I think I have a solution," David said as he dangled his gym bag in the air.

The contents of the gym bag were pulled out between them on the bathroom floor. You had to hand it to David— his gym bag contained the ingredients for three complete outfits even if they were all terrible. The spandex shorts were out because of winter.

Arden pulled the Detroit Tigers sweatshirt over her head. Her black bra slipping beneath the surface a little too quickly. Reese had been too busy rummaging when Arden had slipped her ruined shirt off, which was both professional of her and oddly disappointing.

Reese was taking her time picking through the clothes, trying to decide if she should push Arden to talk about what had upset her before, but she couldn't find a good way into the conversation. Why was this book under so much pressure to get right?

"I don't think you're going to find the perfect outfit in there." Arden was looking down at Reese crouched on the floor, trying to match the electric blue track pants with one of the muscle tees swirling around the bottom of the bag. She glanced at the time on her phone.

"If you're in a hurry to get back, you don't have to wait for me. I can put this hideous outfit together all on my own."

"What would I do without you there? Plus this kind of seems like something I might want to remember later." Arden stifled a laugh as Reese slipped into a spandex muscle T with the words "It's Britney, Bitch" graffitied across it. "Besides, I want to make sure you don't sneak out of the building. I can't really make any progress on the recording without you."

"Well, that's true."

The legs of the pants swept the floor as the pair made their way back to the studio. The flash of Reese's black leather boots peeking out from beneath the blue fabric looked a little unhinged.

As they reached the door Arden's hand wrapped around Reese's wrist. Her grip was firm and warm.

"Did I forget something?" Reese adjusted the now deflated gym bag on her shoulder. They'd left their damp clothes thrown over the bathroom stall doors to dry out.

"No." Arden paused and worried her lower lip. Reese

tried to will herself to look anywhere but at Arden's mouth. "I wanted to say thank you. I know this," she gestured up and down Reese's body, "wasn't your first choice, and I'm still not sure why you agreed to wear these horrible clothes, but I really appreciate it."

Reese followed Arden's gesture, taking in the way the Detroit hoodie fell over her hips. She looked adorable. The familiarity of Arden wearing something with Reese's home-town team on it, the team she still rooted for after moving away, even if it wasn't Reese's sweatshirt, was confusing and exciting all mixed together. Standing there together in the hallway in their sloppy clothes felt intimate. At some point it *had* become her first choice, Reese realized. Watching Arden model men's workout looks in the bathroom trying to make her laugh. And if she'd gone back to her hotel, she wouldn't have had any of this... niceness.

"Sure. These clothes might be ugly, but I am pretty comfortable."

"Well, you look great to me." Arden looked down, a flush rising to her face. "I know I've been feeling a lot of pressure to get this audiobook done, and I think I might have been taking that out on you a bit. I'm not usually so..."

"Uptight?"

"Intense. But uptight works too, I guess." Arden narrowed her eyes at Reese but there was no malice in it. "This project is sort of a comeback for me. A chance to prove I'm back on track." Arden paused, and the silence stretched between them. Her lips parted and then closed again as though she was wrestling with her words.

Reese wanted to ask what Arden meant. Why did people keep hinting that she needed a comeback? And why was she putting this pressure on herself, and Reese by extension, to be perfect?

"Why—"

The creak of the studio door was followed by David's head poking out like a mole. Reese wished she had one of those arcade game mallets so she and Arden could finish their conversation. Reese's arm hit her side with a dull thud. She hadn't realized that Arden had held her wrist that whole time, but now that she'd let go, Reese felt the absence.

"Ready to get rolling? I have to head out early today, so we should get moving. Cute outfits, ladies." David looked back and forth between them with wide eyes. He shot Reese a wink. "Unless you need more alone time." He ducked back into the studio just as Reese went to smack his arm.

DESPITE BEING BURNED by her nice deed and now even more behind schedule, Arden was more pleasant than Reese had ever seen her. She spent most of the morning staring at her computer screen with complete focus. Her typing was a rhythmic white noise that Reese wanted to record and listen to at night.

By the time lunch rolled around, Reese and David had rerecorded the vanished chapters from the night before and then some.

Reese cleared her throat to get Arden's attention, but her typing didn't falter, it sounded gentle like rain against a car window.

Arden removed an earbud, Reese was so used to her noise cancelling headphones that she hadn't even noticed them camouflaged in Arden's dark hair.

"What's good for lunch around here? My treat."

"Really?" Arden looked skeptical.

"You could look a little less surprised. You were nice with coffee. Let me be nice with lunch."

"I thought I burned you with coffee."

Reese lifted up her shirt. The mark from earlier had faded to nothing. "No permanent damage."

Arden licked her lips, and it wasn't lost on Reese that her face fell a bit when she dropped her shirt back down.

Arden called in the order to her favorite coffee shop. Reese double-checked the total and shoved the cash she'd taken out that morning into her pocket; leaving everything else behind.

"Are you sure you don't need help?"

"It's just a couple of salads. I'll be back in a few. You keep working—it looks like you're in the zone."

Arden laughed. "Something like that. I love writing a good make-up sex scene." Arden winked, and Reese felt flames licking her face in response. Time to go.

"Right, that makes, um." What were words and why didn't she know them? "Anyway, I'll be back soon."

———

THE BRASS BELL above the door chimed, announcing her arrival to the beanie-and-ripped-jeans clad customers. Reese quickly looked down at David's too large sweatpants and her black boots and wished desperately for her gross coffee-soaked clothes. Black tacks riddled the wide planks of the floor like studs on a leather jacket. They were taking the distressed thing a little too seriously. Even the floors were cool in a way that made her nervous to walk on them.

The shop was narrow and packed, drink cases scattered amongst mismatched tables and chairs. She took her place at the back of the line that wove through the store. Everyone looked like they were waiting to see a band she'd never heard of.

This coffee shop made her feel not very cool and not very smart. It was bullying her with ambiance.

The line crawled forward and her anxiety inched ahead with it.

"Help you?"

"What?" Reese startled. Had the music just gone from open mic to house party? It was like a weird indie rave all of a sudden, a tambourine stampeding through the speakers.

"Can I help you?" The woman said slowly, her blue lipstick stretching out each word.

"I'm picking up an order."

"What's the name?"

"Reese."

The woman turned around and scanned the paper bags behind her. They looked like the lunches she used to make herself in third grade after her mom left. The ones her classmates made fun of while they ate their tepid French bread pizzas.

"Nothing here by that name."

Reese glanced behind her at the line stretching to the door.

"Maybe it's not ready yet?" The waver of hope in her own voice turned her stomach. This woman's opinion of her didn't matter. A fact Reese understood intellectually that her brain was refusing to convey to her body, which was preparing itself for flight.

The woman called down the counter. "Jace, any orders come in for a Ruth?"

"It's Reese."

"Like the candy?"

"Sure, sort of."

"Any orders for Reese like the candy, Jace?"

"Nope."

The woman looked back at her and shrugged. Was this some sort of speakeasy? Was she not cool enough to get the password for some arugula?

The woman was wearing obscenely short jean cutoffs over black leggings—an interesting choice for winter. Someone who couldn't dress themselves should not be this intimidating. She looked down at the sweats and fancy boots. Case in point.

"Can you try Arden? My friend ordered it." Friend was a stretch, but saying it sent a warm jolt through Reese. She made a note to examine that later.

She turned from Reese and rustled through the bags again. "Here you go." Her statement was punctuated by two paper bags dropped onto the counter. Both said Arden in intricate, swooping black sharpie underlined by little vines —a little excessive for labeling during lunch rush, but that did explain why the line was so slow.

"The total is $62.72. Put your card in whenever you're ready." The woman spun a tablet toward Reese, and she resisted the urge to swat it back. Her fist tightened around the cash in her pocket. The cash that was definitely not enough. How had the order increased more than $20 on her walk over? Inflation? In this economy?

"I think there's a mistake. The total when we ordered was $37.42."

She watched the woman wave someone else over as they had a whispered conversation.

"Someone called and changed the order. We have a note here."

. . .

THE DÉJÀ VU crashed into her, Reese was eight again looking at the total on the register at the corner store and trying to stack the bills and coins in her hands so they'd add up. But just like when she jumped for the peanut butter on the top shelf, she could never quite reach. She always needed an adult to get it for her, or more often they'd go without. She put the package of American cheese on top of the rack of gum and the cashier swiped it and tossed it aside, shaking her head.

"Do you want this left out?" The woman said, shaking Lo's bag of M&Ms like a maraca.

She nodded.

After that they ate butter sandwiches for a week, until her dad's next disability check came in.

BUT SHE WASN'T eight anymore; she wouldn't be returning to her butter sandwich days. She'd constructed her entire life to never have to go back there. Of course Arden was the kind of person who would call and order more expensive food. Reese squirmed as the eyes of the restless customers behind her sparked off her back.

She scanned the menu, but her eyes wouldn't focus. The items were written in scrolling white chalk taunting her like the Arden on the bag. The letters swam when she squinted. All menus should be organized by price, lowest to highest, so she could just point and get what she could afford.

"Can I change the order again? Sorry, it's just I only brought cash and I don't—"

"Sure. What do you want to change?" The woman asked without glancing up from her phone.

"Can I change the salad for a plain bagel? That's $1, right?"

"Bagels are $7, they come with cream cheese."

That was obscene. Was the cream cheese from a golden cow? She took a deep breath. She was an adult, not some helpless kid anymore. She could manage this.

"Ok, but how much for a plain one?"

"Seven dollars."

Nothing made sense in this fucking city.

"Fine, no bagel and no Mediterranean salad. What is it then?"

The woman sighed and tapped the tablet screen. "$36.43."

"Ok, great." Reese clenched her jaw and handed over the two twenties she'd brought.

The woman took them and shoved them into her apron pocket. In one smooth motion she pushed one of the bags toward Reese and the other off the side of the counter. Her lunch thunked as it hit the bottom of the trash can. "We don't make change."

SIX

The walk back to the studio had not calmed her rage. It raced through her like a house fire, singeing everything it touched. She clutched the brown bag holding Arden's absurdly expensive lunch, her fingers icicle cold and ready to snap. It gave "pry it from my cold dead hands" a whole new meaning.

How dare Arden put her in that position? And even worse, how dare she do that to herself? The whole way back she carried Arden's lunch while hers was getting a slow coffee ground burial in the trash at the mean girl coffee shop.

Arden was focused on her computer, her hair thrown up in a messy bun secured with a pencil. The Detroit hoodie was draped over the back of her chair. She had a tattoo on the back of her arm that looked like lavender delicately inching its way to her shoulder. Reese hated that she loved it. Hated that it made her wonder what other tattoos there were to discover.

Tattoos were like a scavenger hunt. Clues revealed slowly over time until at the end you discovered their meaning, how they all came together, what they told you about the person. Well, Reese wouldn't be finding out anything else about Arden if she could help it.

Reese tossed the brown bag of food onto the table. It slid to a stop against Arden's computer with a satisfying thud. She jumped back from her computer like it was an animal ready to pounce. It wasn't the animal she needed to be afraid of. Reese's anger was feral. Her heartbeat crackled in her ears.

Arden pushed her glasses back up her nose with her index finger, her dark eyes blinked as though to make sense of what was happening. It was damn near disarming. But forgiving people, too quickly or at all, was how Reese spent years of her life having her heart broken over and over again.

Arden smiled like nothing was wrong, and it made something thrash inside Reese's chest. She struggled to keep her face passive, like a rodeo cowboy trying to control something wild and unruly. If she tried to smile she'd gnash her teeth. If she tried to be nice right now, her anger would throw her to the dirt and trample her.

"Thanks," Arden said, dragging out the word as she narrowed her eyes. As though if she waited long enough she would make sense of Reese. When she squinted like that her eyes were black as space.

Reese bit her lower lip until it felt like her teeth were about to meet. She fought to hold her anger close, she didn't want it to float away in whatever zero gravity effect Arden's eyes were having on her.

"Everything ok?"

Arden's voice was soft, and the kindness in it spurred Reese's rage. How could Arden be so careless and then insult her by not having any idea what position she'd put her in?

"Yup." Reese grabbed her wallet and turned on her heel ready to walk back out and find a food cart.

"Would you want to eat together? My agent had to cancel for today so I can take a break. I know yesterday didn't go so well, but I promise no notes today, just food." Arden's smile was so nice and a little crooked like she was feeling unsure.

"I don't have lunch." Reese's molars felt about to crack under the pressure she was putting on them. If the agent cancelled, she could have gone to her hotel and showered. She could be in her own clothes. Neither of those things were Arden's fault, but Reese's rage was holding her 100% responsible.

"What do you mean? We just got lunch."

"It was more expensive than they said on the phone and I only took so much cash. So, I didn't get anything."

"Oh." Arden's brows furrowed "Oh, shit. Because I changed my order."

"Yup."

The color drained from Arden's face. She looked like she wanted to cover her eyes and watch the rest of this conversation through the cracks between her fingers.

"I'm sorry, I didn't realize it would cause a problem."

"Yeah, obviously." Reese hated the edge in her voice, sharpened from years of similar experiences. Of being let down. Of being put in a bad position. Of being blindsided by the selfishness of others. She longed for her apartment where the door was always locked, and the only one who ever let her down was the mailman.

"I get that you're upset and I'm sorry, but I had to change the order."

"It was careless. It felt so—you know what? It doesn't matter."

"Reese, wait. Don't do that. Clearly it does matter. But it wasn't careless. I told you I had to change it. The other one had something I can't have. Why didn't you call me? I could have come to meet you. This didn't have to be a big deal."

Did Arden have a point? Reese tried to picture this utopian world Arden imagined where this wasn't a big deal but she couldn't.

"No, just because it's not a big deal to you, doesn't mean it's not a big deal. That's the problem, you think everything revolves around you. But it doesn't. I'm going to go get lunch, and then when I come back I'm going to do my job and record your book, so we can get this over with."

REESE WAS face down on her bed, arms and legs extended like a skydiver.

"So how bad are we talking?"

Lo's voice was tinny coming out of her phone's speaker.

"I yelled at her and stormed out."

"What was that? You sound like you're covering your mouth."

Reese lifted her head from the mattress and let it fall back, her forehead bouncing slightly. She let out a loud sigh as she rolled onto her side to face the phone.

"Now that sigh I heard." Lo's laugh cut through the quiet room and Reese felt the smile tugging at her face in a Pavlovian response.

"Ugh, I feel like I have a hangover from my bad behavior. Do you ever get those?"

"I usually feel like I have a hangover because I *have* a hangover. So, no."

"Well, something for you to aspire to, then. Do you think I can blame it on being hungry?"

"The old hangry defense? That could work. Or you could just explain why it upset you so much."

"Because it was careless and selfish."

"No, not why you're telling yourself it upset you, but why it really did."

"Wow, a few weeks of therapy in rehab and suddenly you're hanging up your shingle."

"What is this approach? Hair of the dog with the bad behavior? Just keep that buzz going, so you don't have to deal with the fallout? Huh, I guess I am getting good at this therapy stuff. Aren't you glad I'm getting my money's worth this time? If there's one thing I learned it's that you'll never be faster than your past. It will always catch you."

"Ok, that's our 50 minutes, Dr. Lo." Reese loved her sister, but she didn't like her when she tried to analyze a conversation.

"Ok, I'll stop. After I say this—"

Reese groaned, but Lo didn't pause.

"You're only in New York for a few weeks. It's an adventure. And nothing you've told me about Arden sounds as bad as you've decided she is. Give her another chance."

Reese felt the response that it was her money scratch at her throat—it was a sneeze she tried painfully to suppress.

Why the hell did Lo have to go and get so insightful? She had a job to do and a life to get back to, but there wasn't any reason she couldn't make the best of her time in New York, even if the streets were a swirling pit of chaos.

SEVEN

"Cut!"

Reese closed her eyes to keep from rolling them. She'd lost track of how many times she'd been corrected by the infallible Arden Abbott today, and they still had two hours left on the meter.

"This isn't a film you're directing, Arden. I'm reading the words *you* wrote. And maybe if you let me do that, you could see that I know what I'm doing, and we could make some progress."

Reese was using her bedtime story voice, calm as a sleep meditation. It soothed her even if it wasn't working to calm down the one person in the studio who really needed to chill the fuck out.

"This one isn't minor." Arden paced the studio—three steps, about face, three steps. She had the energy of a wrecking ball about to demolish Reese. You're saying 'and' like 'end'. This isn't some Wisconsin cheese commercial."

"No, I'm not. And that is the definition of minor. I'm saying 'and' normally, like everyone says it all across America."

Reese looked to David for backup, but he was focused on his soundboard, adjusting dials seemingly at random.

"Say it again then. We can vote."

"Nope, I'm not going to say it just to be criticized. Who are you to be voting on how I say words? I'm the resident professional word-sayer around here. Besides, David is obligated to take my side, I have dirt on him going all the way back to third grade when he used to eat it."

A smile played at Arden's lips. "Ok Ms. Professional word-sayer, if you're so sure I'm wrong, then what's the problem?"

Reese shrugged and released the smile she'd been biting back. "I think it would be embarrassing for you and seeing that happen to people makes me feel bad. I'm not sure if you're aware, but I'm a very empathetic person."

David barked out a laugh and then mouthed "I'm sorry" in Reese's direction before averting his eyes.

"You really think you can get through the rest of the day without saying and?"

"Anything's possible when you believe in yourself."

"David, darling," Arden's voice had the lilt of someone enjoying this very much, "play back that last part for Reese to hear."

David had the good sense to avoid Reese's glare as he cued up the recording. His face crunched in painful concentration as he pressed buttons.

Listening to her own voice was her least favorite part of her job. But listening to herself *with* an audience was a brand-new circle of hell. She swallowed down the wave of nausea that crashed against her ribs.

Reese usually squirmed her way through edits before turning in completed audio files for a book. One of the benefits of this job in New York was supposed to be that she didn't have to listen to herself say things like "I want you to fuck me so hard I—Sarah brought her finger to my lips, and I took it into my mouth. When she groaned, I felt it between my thighs."

But she wasn't going to back down on this one. She wouldn't cover her ears or walk out even if it was against-the-Geneva-conventions-literal torture. Reese had been capitulating to Arden all day, and it was only making her stronger and more insufferable. So, if ending this meant listening to herself beg for it in a tiny room with a beautiful, terrible woman and her oldest friend, then that's what she'd do. Because she was a damn professional.

"Fine," Reese met Arden's eye and winked. "Roll the tape."

The satisfied look on Arden's face told her everything she needed to know. Reese hated to be wrong, and she hated the way Arden lit up when she was right. And she hated the glimmer in her dark eyes that she'd never seen before and how sexy and smug the combination was. And she really, really hated that she noticed a single thing about her.

"Ok, so I say 'end', not 'and'. There's nothing wrong with a midwestern accent. Many people find them charming."

"Oh, I find your accent charming."

"Oh," Reese stopped short. Had Arden really called her charming? "Thanks, I don't get that a lot and—"

"Charming and totally wrong for this character."

"Yup, there it is."

"Reese, can you try to understand that I just want this book to be perfect and do well? I have a lot riding on it."

"I understand that, *Arden*. And I'm working hard to make that happen even if I am finding this process infuriating. But do you really think people are buying your book for the ands?"

"Among other words."

"You're impossible." Reese couldn't remember the last time she had been so thoroughly challenged at every turn. Another benefit of keeping to herself. She was surprised to find the sparring bordering on enjoyable. "I'm going to take five to go scream into the void. When I get back you can explain to me how to say 'and'."

"Like the name Ann but with a d."

"Bye, Arden." Reese held in her laugh as she headed for the door. Better not to show her hand until she could organize the cards herself.

REESE HESITATED outside the door of the studio. Arden was standing in the far corner, pinned in by a small woman dressed in a skirt suit like a thrift store couch: the color of tapioca pudding with iridescent bubble gum pink threads running through it. The fabric looked about as soft as steel wool, a scouring pad from a 1960s kitchen.

Her phone buzzed in her pocket. Another text from Judith with two blurry plant photos and a string of rainbow hearts. She sent a thumbs up and shut the screen off. The phone buzzed out its call pattern. When would she learn not to reply to Judith's texts right away? That woman was all about the immediate follow-up call.

She considered hitting ignore and sending a sorry can't talk text. But what if this time there was an emergency? "Hi, Judith."

"Reese! I can't believe you answered. How's the big apple? Have you been to Times Square? You could take some pictures with those characters like the toy cowboy for your website."

Had Judith ever been on her website? Or the internet in general? "I haven't gone to Times Square. As you can imagine, crowds aren't really my thing."

"Oh, you poor thing. Of course they aren't. Are you doing ok there? Is there anything there you like?"

"I like bookstores and museums." And the silence of her hotel bath, but she didn't need Judith to misinterpret her blissful alone time and feel sorry for her.

"Well, museums are good, too. Maybe you can take a picture with a pterodactyl instead."

"Yeah, sure." A picture with a pterodactyl actually didn't sound like the worst idea she'd ever heard. "Is everything ok? I'm working right now."

The couch lady was pointing at Arden, and Reese was rooting for Arden to swat her hand like a tetherball. For once she was disappointed that voices weren't carrying outside of the soundproof studio.

"I have some bad news." Judith's voice dropped to that irresistible whisper of someone about to gossip in church. Reese tuned in immediately. "I overwatered your aloe plant. It looks fine, but I was reading a plant book and it said it should only ge—"

"That's fine, I'm sure you didn't hurt anything." Reese watched Arden cross her arms. At least things were moving in the right direction—confrontation wise. "You probably don't need to water them anymore while I'm gone."

"Ok, dear. I'll just go in and check the soil. I actually just bought this thing at DeVine's on Michigan Avenue to check the moisture level—it's sort of like a meat thermometer."

"Oh, that's, well..." Reese tried to focus on the conversation with Judith instead of trying to guess what Arden and this lady were saying. "That's actually really nice of you. Maybe you can show me how to use it when I get back."

"I'd love to! We can go to the store together—you'd love it, lots of prickly plants."

"Sure, that sounds fine." The woman was pulling up something on her phone and showing it to Arden. Arden grimaced like the screen gave her heartburn.

"Really? That's incredible, when will you be home? We could pick a date now."

"Let's do that later, things are still a little uncertain here. Look I have to go. Thanks for calling, Judith."

"Ok dear, call anytime."

THE COOL METAL of the door handle was grasped in Reese's palm before she considered what she was doing.

She stepped to one side until she was sure she'd cut off the angle for Arden to see her from the studio. She eased open the door a millimeter at a time, holding her breath to preserve the silence. She felt like a kid again in the days before her mom left, stealthily eavesdropping on her parents' arguments.

"You can't afford to mess this up, Arden. I'm sure I don't need to remind you that I stuck by you when no one else did. I really need you to get the recording back on track. Remember we're going for reliability. Everyone is taking a chance on trusting you again."

"I know that. I'll fix it." Arden was slouched like a balloon that had lost too much air to float and now hovered at kicking height. Reese had never seen her look so deflated, not even yesterday during the coffee incident. What the hell did this woman have on her?

"Good. Now, how's writing going?"

"It's slow, but it's coming. I was thinking this next one could be more of a novella. I want to write about someone in recovery finding love, but I'm not sure I could sustain it for a full-length novel at this point."

"Your readers don't want that—it's too heavy. Why don't you write about a florist who finds love at a wedding she's working at?" The woman's voice was gravel under a luxury vehicle; there was a bite to its moneyed purr.

Oh, so this woman wanted Arden to just lift the plot of the holy grail of lesbian rom-coms? Great suggestion, couch lady. What Arden described sounded like *exactly* the kind of book Reese would want to read *and* record. Though not one she'd imagined Arden would want to write. When Lo got sober she started to realize how few books talk about sobriety. And how very many use a drunken night to lower inhibitions and push the characters together. Was there any way she could tell Arden that without leading with 'when I was spying on you and that Jackie O wannabe'?

"That's been done, Sophia."

Reese was rooting for the woman to turn around even if it meant getting caught being slightly, just a teeny bit, unprofessional by eavesdropping. Didn't agents work *for* the clients they represented? The power dynamic between Arden and Sophia was like a seesaw with a davenport on one side and a decent person on the other.

Sophia threw her arms up, but they stopped at shoulder level in a T. Her jacket wasn't just terrible, it was also a size too small.

"You're the expert on that Arden, not me. Maybe a wedding photographer then, whatever. But I promise no one wants to read about addiction in their romances. Why don't you show me your outline, and I'll make some suggestions to get you back on track? I can probably save what you have, just cut out the sad stuff. You know what they say, writing is re-writing."

"I don't think that's what that saying means."

"Irregardless. Like I said you're the expert. But I promise no one wants to read about addiction in a romance. This is why you pay me the big bucks."

"I'll email it to you later."

"I'll wait while you email it now. That way you can get back to work tonight instead of wasting more time on something I can't sell. Romance is supposed to be *happy* even if you aren't."

Arden looked like she'd been slapped. Her cheeks glowed pink. "Fine."

A well of protectiveness rose up in Reese, and she understood how firefighters must feel when they run into a burning building. She wanted to throw Arden over her shoulder and pull her out of that room.

"Great. Now tell me how the audiobook is going."

"We're trying to make sure it's perfect. Reese has been great."

"If she's so great why are you two days behind schedule?"

"We had some hiccups early on, but we're good now."

"Glad to hear it. When you call me later, I want to hear that you've hit double today's goals."

"I don't think that's going to happen. We only have a few hours left and then I was going to go to a meeting tonight—I kind of need it."

"I still don't understand why you waste your time at those things. Listening to all those sad stories when you could be writing. You're fine now, and if you let those stories make you sad then *your* stories will be sad, and no one will like them. It's called happily ever after for a reason."

"Happily just refers to the ever after—the ending. Most of the story is about the journey, the struggle toward growth."

"Fine. Do what you want but hit your goals first. Getting you back on top is my priority, and it should be yours too."

That's what she said. How was Arden not hitting this terrible lady with hair like a Swiffer duster with that comeback?

Reese eased the door closed and started down the hallway in the opposite direction. Desperate to put some space between herself and the studio. The person Arden had been in that conversation was not the Arden who had been giving her a hard time for days. She was like a jack-o-lantern with its candle blown out, a sad decapitated squash. Reese needed to be more careful not to smash her.

EIGHT

Reese had a good feeling about today. After the progress they'd made yesterday the project was sort of, almost, kind of back on track. Plus, not a single person had disturbed her last night—not Judith's plant emergencies, or unexpected hotel room visitors. Though part of Reese felt a little disappointed about that last one.

This happened about once a year. She woke up feeling ready for whatever the world threw her way. Lo called them her halcyon days because she said it was like Reese was too young and naive to know that everything's terrible. Not that she had ever been that naive, she'd been born a jaded octogenarian, but on days like today it felt like something worthy to aspire to.

The sun was streaming through the buildings, warming the sidewalk. One of those rare March days that feels like a preview of spring. Reese handed the coffee cart vendor exact change and inhaled steam from the blue paper cup that didn't even smell too burnt. A pigeon swooped in front of her and its feathers were iridescent, as a driveway oil spot in the morning light.

No matter what happened today, she'd be in a good mood about it. No matter how many times Arden derailed her reading, she would not let it get to her. Her frustration with Arden had become more elusive—it was like smoke, still visible but harder to hold on to after seeing her talk to her agent yesterday. Since she'd arrived in New York, she'd never seen Arden look anything other than totally confident, but yesterday she had looked small.

Something about the way that woman had spoken to Arden—her dismissiveness—had made Reese want to cover her in bubble wrap. She spent longer than she'd ever admit last night trying not to think about that feeling too much. She'd also spent a long time googling Arden, trying to unlock the mystery of why she was so hard on herself. There were a few vague references to a failed movie deal and a delayed book, but nothing she found went into detail. Which was for the best—googling someone she knew felt creepy.

Sure, she and Arden bickered, and she was hands down the most infuriating person she'd ever met—besides Judith— but that didn't mean she disliked Arden. She just wanted her to relax. To stop being so obsessed with perfection that she sucked everyone around her into the vortex of it. And she wanted to be left alone to record the book so she could get paid, dig herself out of this financial hole, then retreat to her apartment forever. Now she had the added motivation of wanting this book to be perfect so Arden's agent would let her live her life.

She was so in her head that she almost ran straight into David. He was standing on the street in front of the studio, his head thrown back tilting his face toward the sky. The sun bounced off his glasses.

She braced a hand on his shoulder to steady herself. Not a drop of coffee was lost. "Good morning! It's a beautiful day to save this project, don't you think?"

"Reese? Is that you? I can't see you through that blinding ray of enthusiasm."

"I'm allowed to be in a good mood."

"Sure you are. You've just never shown any interest in that in the past."

"Ha ha. Anyway, do you have any plans this weekend? Would you want to go to the library with me? Or something more fun like the Morbid Anatomy Museum? I've been in New York almost a week, and I'm slightly reconsidering spending so much of it alone in my hotel room. Maybe I need to explore the city."

"One, you hate the city. Two, your ideas of fun are the library and a museum with morbid in the name? Come here, let me see if you have a fever. I think you might be on actual fire."

She ducked as David shot his hand out.

"I'm fine. So what do you say? I'm feeling bold, but I'd rather not navigate the subway alone. That thing is like an Indiana Jones movie: haunted and full of fun ways to die. I've read good things about the museum—it's a popup exhibit at Green-Wood Cemetery through the end of the month."

"I have no interest in going to a morbid pop-up museum at a cemetery in winter, Reesey. I love you, but that's pushing it. Coney Island on Saturday—it should be deserted and a little depressing—it's no macabre graveyard, but it should still be perfect for you."

"What are you two standing outside for?"

"Just enjoying the morning!" Reese turned to Arden and smiled.

Arden raised an eyebrow. "I'm sorry, are you in a good mood?"

"Weird, but it happens." Reese studied her. With the sun reflecting off the buildings and radiating behind her, Arden glowed. She looked perfect. Tired, but perfect. She was dressed down in dark jeans and a zip up gray hoodie with a white shirt peeking out from underneath. There was something classic and effortless about it, and it made Reese feel like a Sunday full of endless hours for brunch and crosswords.

"Okay," Arden said, slowly stretching the two syllables out. "Were you two just talking about the Morbid Museum at Green-Wood? You should definitely go. I went last weekend. It's got a lot of interesting stuff."

David widened his eyes at Reese as he looked between her and Arden. When Arden turned toward him, he dropped the look from his face.

Reese did a double-take. Was it possible Arden had interests beyond making the book perfect? And did those interests actually intersect with hers?

"That's so interesting, Arden." David's voice was ebbing into its highest register, and Reese felt her apprehension rising with it. "Reese was just saying how badly she wants to go this weekend, but unfortunately I have plans. Since you've already been, and Reese doesn't really know her way around, maybe you two could go? I'd feel better knowing she has a buddy there in case she gets scared of all the mummies or whatever."

Reese shot David a glare. "I'm not going to get scared," Reese said at the same time Arden spoke. "Sorry, Arden. What were you saying?"

"I was saying I'd love to. I didn't get to stay as long as I wanted last weekend because I got too cold."

"Oh, ok. As long as you don't feel obligated." Was she seriously going to spend time with Arden outside of recording? She tried to push down the spike of excitement that flowed through her veins.

"Not at all."

"That could be ok, I guess." Was her voice shaking? Reese took a sip of her coffee to hide her shock and give her body a minute to calm down.

"Don't sound too eager," Arden said sarcastically. "It's just a walk through a cemetery, not a proposal."

"What is it with you and bringing up proposals?" A smile played at the edge of her mouth. Over Arden's shoulder, she caught David's confused look. "Though it would be hard to say no to a cemetery proposal."

Arden quirked an eyebrow. "Good to know."

Reese liked this side of Arden. It felt more alive, less robotic. Maybe she was having a halcyon day too. Teasing Arden made Reese feel warm. And it was nice to not have Arden correcting everything she did. Maybe a little premature to call that seeing as they hadn't yet started recording for the day. There were still plenty of hours for Reese to say things with a strange but barely detectable accent.

It definitely wouldn't be terrible to have someone to look at the exhibits with. Someone who wouldn't squirm the entire time like David would. Someone who just happened to be very pretty and currently smiling at her. How had she never noticed that dimple on Arden's right cheek before? How was she ever able to focus on anything else. Probably because Reese had never done much to make her smile.

"Great then, that's settled." Arden rubbed her hands

together. "So, back to my original question, why is everyone standing on the sidewalk?"

Reese looked around. She was right. It wasn't just David standing on the sidewalk enjoying his coffee—the entire building seemed to be outside thumbing through their phones with various degrees of distress clouding their features.

"Just enjoying the sunshine, I thought." Reese looked to David for confirmation.

Arden looked at Reese with her brows knit together. It made Reese feel like a Picasso painting, features askew.

"I never would have guessed I'd find you two outside enjoying the morning."

"Well actually, that's just why Reese is outside. I'm outside because someone set off the fire alarm and the sprinklers went off inside."

"What?" Reese and Arden's voices overlapped in alarm, but Arden's frantically won out. "Is everything ok? Is the equipment damaged? What does it mean for the schedule?"

"Why didn't you say anything?"

"I didn't want to ruin your good mood, Reese. Plus, there's nothing we can do until we get the all-clear from the fire department before we can get back in. Then I need to check everything. The sprinklers were going off on our floor, so I was going to see if I can get them to rip up the carpet today, so we don't have to deal with that noise when recording."

"So, we're fucked?"

The laugh bubbling in Reese's throat escaped before she could stop it and both David and Arden turned to look at her.

"Sorry. I don't think I've ever heard Arden swear. It was nice."

"This good mood is weird on you. I'm not sure I trust it." But Arden's slight smile took some of the sting out of her words.

"Well, luckily for everyone it doesn't come around too often."

"Yeah," David confirmed, "it's like leap year frequency. Nothing to worry about."

"I feel like I'm always just outside of some secret club you two are in. Like I'm staring up at your treehouse listening to you laugh about me."

"No one's laughing at you. Ok, the fire marshal is giving the all-clear. I'm going to head in and see what needs to be done. I'm guessing we're in for a day of loud repair noises and I'm not sure recording is worth it. Let's call it a day and I'll reach out later if we can be back to work tomorrow."

"But what about—"

"The schedule. I know, Arden. Let's plan on working Saturday to make up the time? Reese, this means we can't do Coney Island."

David's eyes flashed and Reese saw what was coming. She wanted to leap in front of it, anything to stop this kamikaze move.

"Maybe Arden can take you to Coney Island? Since you two both have the day off." The smile on David's face was clown wide. Reese was trying to murder him with her eyes.

"Arden probably has writing she can do today anyway. I can just go by myself."

"Please, we both know when you leave here, you're just going to sit alone at your hotel."

That's it, David was officially fired as her best friend.

"I'd love a day off, actually. I was up writing most of the

night. I mean, if you don't mind the company." Arden looked down at her boots scuffing one against the sidewalk.

She seemed almost... nervous. This day was getting stranger by the minute.

"Great! That settles it. I'll be here working my butt off, getting the studio back together and you two can go off and enjoy each other...'s company."

Reese raised an eyebrow at David from behind Arden's back and made the universal throat-slitting motion.

"Just beware—Reese cheats at arcade games. Don't let her innocent face fool you. She's cutthroat."

Arden laughed and caught Reese's eye. "I think I'm up to the challenge."

CONEY ISLAND WAS A GHOST TOWN. Of course, everything was closed at an outdoor amusement park in the winter. It made perfect sense. And it had not occurred to Reese once. The lack of crowd she'd expected, the locked gates not so much.

She pulled her leather jacket more tightly around her and glanced over at Arden. Arden was shivering in the wind, her hoodie useless against the sea spray coming off the ocean each time the wind blew.

Another thing Reese had forgotten to factor in was how much colder everything was near the water. The sun kept slipping behind clouds like it was a boxer bobbing and weaving around the ring.

"Remind me again why you wanted to come here?" Arden crossed her arms tightly across her chest. But an amused smile was pulling at the corner of her mouth and that cute dimple was back on her right cheek. She almost looked like she wasn't about to murder Reese in a bout of freezing temporary insanity and roll her body into the bay they were approaching.

"Because I love carnival games and the ocean, and I couldn't pass up a chance to walk down Mermaid Avenue. And also, I forgot everything would be closed."

Arden's laugh was magical, like the first time you hear the ocean inside a shell. "Everything's closed because it's fucking freezing out and no sane person wants to be on the Ferris Wheel overlooking the ocean right now. Aren't you cold?"

Reese shook her head. "Nope, I'm good." It was cold out here, objectively, with the wind whipping off of the water. But even as the chill sliced through her leather jacket, Reese was reluctant to end their time together.

"Liar. You literally shivered as you said that." Arden said with her own shudder.

"Just by association. I actually run really warm."

"You're cold by association?"

"Yup. It's like yawning. Inexplicably contagious. See I'm fine." Arden's skin was soft beneath Reese's palm when she held her hand to Arden's cheek, proving her point. If Reese's act surprised her, Arden didn't show it. She leaned into the gesture like a cat accepting attention.

"How are your hands that warm? Mine are literally frozen." Arden pulled one of her hands from her pocket.

Reese was still admiring Arden's hands. Her nail polish was the same color as the space between the stars, and it stood out against the blueish tint of her cold hands. Maybe she did mean literally. The nail polish choice felt nostalgic and like a shooting star, a memory flashed across Reese's mind—kissing her first girlfriend, who wasn't her girlfriend at all, at a loud rock show in some sticky club basement, xmarked hands gripping waists and beer pooling around their feet like a rising tide.

Arden shot her hand out and let her fingers trail along the back of Reese's neck, sending chills down her spine.

Reese slapped her hand over Arden's and tried to pull it away. Anything to stop the feeling of an ice cube sliding down her neck. Arden danced her fingers away and laughed until Reese was able to lace their fingers together and pull their joint hands down between them.

Reese's fingers protested. She could have been holding iced coffee in the snow for as cold as Arden's fingers felt in hers. But she found it hard to let go, as if their hands had frozen together and the splitting of them would be delicate and painful. Better not chance it.

It felt nice, too. Arden's hand in hers. It had been a long time since she'd held someone's hand. Since she'd found someone's company enjoyable.

It's not that she didn't have her share of hookups. Dating apps had made that all very convenient. And she did a lot of things involving hands on those nights, but somehow this seemed more intimate than all of them put together. *But was it? There was nothing intimate between her and Arden. Up until a few days ago, there was hardly even tolerance.*

Reese pulled her hand away and shoved it into her coat pocket. Arden's hand dropped to her side with a slight thud.

"It's like this in Chicago too, always colder at Navy Pier on the water."

"Oh right, you have that big lake."

'That big lake' was the perfect way to describe Lake Michigan, which stretched out vast and ocean-like between Illinois and its namesake's lower peninsula. It was hard to explain how big the Great Lakes are to someone who's never stood on their shores, humbled as they watch the freshwater waves in the stormy blue waters crashing into the horizon and disappearing.

"I'm impressed you're not panicking about the schedule delay, or, if you are you're hiding it well."

Arden laughed and held her hands up. "I'm not hiding anything. Between us, it's kind of nice to take a break I can't be blamed for. The pace has been intense."

Reese tilted her head to the side, wondering if she'd heard Arden right. But she decided not to challenge her. "Ok, I think I've tortured you enough. Ready to get out of the cold so I can beat you at skeeball?"

"I didn't even realize skeeball could be competitive," Arden said, bumping her shoulder into Reese's.

Reese felt a flash where their shoulders touched like two rocks sparking together. She was suddenly very glad that David was stuck at the studio.

"You're about to learn a lot, Abbott."

"Nope, hard pass. Let's stick with Arden."

"How about Denny?"

"Medium pass. No one's called me that since high school. You don't want me to return to my emo days."

"Ok, full names only. But suddenly the nail polish makes more sense."

Arden laughed. "You hate it?"

"No, I don't. It reminds me of being young and making bad decisions."

"Wow, thanks." Arden narrowed her eyes.

"I mean bad decisions in a good way." And she meant it. Arden struck Reese as someone who had made her fair share of bad decisions but had still managed to find her way to solid ground. Reese liked that bit of darkness around the edges.

"Do you want to keep digging, or do you want to get out your phone and get us a ride to this penny arcade? The best one I know is a few miles from here."

"Fine, I guess I can always go back to digging later."

Reese took her phone from her jacket pocket. She opened google but the reception out by the water was almost nonexistent.

"Order a car? Like takeout?" She looked up and down the street in an exaggerated way meant to hide her very real confusion. The street was empty as summer tourist traps in the middle of winter are destined to be. She knew apps like this existed but she'd never had much occasion to use one because she never left her apartment. They had weird names like ReV and SPNtR.

"No, like a rideshare. Did they ban those in Chicago or something? You don't strike me as someone who takes the train everywhere."

"Of course, I was just kidding. I'll get a car. And you're right, I don't take the train anywhere. I work from home, so..." Reese decided to leave out the part about never leaving her apartment.

"That makes sense."

Reese fiddled with her phone for several minutes scrolling through the results of her search. Arden peered over her shoulder and Reese could feel the glow of her sideways grin.

"What are you doing over there? Downloading one? Here, I'll do it."

Arden moved to grab her phone, and Reese extended her arm straight up into the air. She had maybe an inch and a half on Arden in these boots, and she was currently using every centimeter of it.

Arden stopped struggling to reach it. Reese had never felt more smug about a footwear choice.

"Did you really google 'how to get a ride'? Do you not have any rideshare apps? Also, you should turn on filters, so your searches are a little more, um, relevant."

Reese widened her eyes. "How did you—"

"If you wanted to hide it, you shouldn't have kept the screen facing me."

Reese held up her hands in surrender. "Ok fine. I'm bad at this. I don't have any of those apps. First I had to google rideshare apps and now I'm reading reviews to find the best one."

"The best one is Lyft. I'm freezing to death, and you're leaving me like Jack in the water as you read app ratings from the comfort of your floating door."

"I just wanted to get the right one! I've never used them before, and I was trying to feel *less* embarrassed about that by picking a good one."

"Wait, what? I'm not trying to be stuck on this, but you live in a city, how do you not have this already? How have you never taken a Lyft?"

"I don't go out much. I guess I like where I live."

"Sure, I walk around my neighborhood, but what about when you need to go to another part of the city? I know Chicago's smaller than New York, but it's not exactly walkable. How do you get across town or to concerts?"

"I haven't been to a concert in awhile. I guess I took a cab to the last one?"

"What was the last concert you went to?"

"Have you heard of The Shrikes?"

"I've seen them live three times! Did Zoey sing Midnight solo? She did when I saw them, it was so intimate.

That's not that long—Kaleidoscope is still a pretty new album."

"The last concert I went to was for their first album—Heart's Content."

"Oh. That was... a very long time ago."

Reese nodded as she did some quick math that told her before taking this job she hadn't left her apartment in 272 days. A glorious streak. "Yeah, it's been a little while." She focused on opening her phone and hoped the wind chill was masking the blush on her face. Freezing and embarrassed are close cousins. Even though she had nothing to be embarrassed about. Her life was fine. Good, even. Some days she bordered on happy.

Leaving her apartment was objectively terrible at best and actively traumatizing at worst. People were the reason she didn't get up some mornings. These truths are self-evident. And besides, why should she care what Arden Abbott thinks? Soon enough she'd be back in Chicago, and Arden would be in New York, and all of this would be a memory.

NINE

"So, let me get this straight." Reese was trying to make sense of things as they waited for their ride. "You use this app to let a complete stranger know you're stranded, *and* you give them your exact location? I just think we're making a murderer's job too easy. We definitely shouldn't be paying them for this."

"You're ridiculous," Arden said as she brushed her shoulder into Reese's. "What is taking this guy so long?"

"Yes, I, too, wish he'd hurry up and kill us."

They heard the car before they saw it. Its bass rattling their eardrums. The lowrider was the sparkly deep cherry red of a hot wheels car. It caught the faint rays of the sun and rebounded each one, a moving disco ball slowly approaching the curb. There were honest-to-god flames above the wheel wells.

Reese quirked an eyebrow at Arden. Surely walking was better.

"It's an adventure," Arden shrugged. She opened the long front door and it swung out over the sidewalk, almost taking out Reese's knees. Arden pulled a lever that flipped the front seat forward. A narrow gap appeared for passage into the dark cave of the back seat. It looked like one of those plastic tunnels that kids love to play in—the kind that grab your hair and trap you in awkward army crawling positions. Like crawling through a sewer only definitely more germs and branded as fun.

"Your chariot, M'lady," Arden whispered, a laugh just beneath the surface as she bowed deeply and made a princely sweeping gesture with her arm.

Making adults climb into the back seat of a two-door car should be a punishable offense. There is no world in which she wasn't about to look like a total fool in front of Arden.

Reese clattered into the back seat, her arms swinging for purchase. She tumbled onto the white leather, relieved but not proud of her performance. She didn't *want* to care if she looked good in front of Arden but in that moment she really, really did.

Reese slid over behind the driver to make room for Arden.

"Fuck," she whispered as her knees crashed into her chest. She tried again to Tetris them behind his nearly horizontal seat, desperately wanting to avoid contact.

How could an adult man drive in this position? How does he even see the road? He was reclined so much that he might as well have been sitting in a La-Z-Boy to rest his eyes during half time instead of driving *safely* and *efficiently* around the world's biggest city.

Arden slid in gracefully beside her and pulled the door closed. When she pulled the front-seat back into place, Reese felt like the bar had just come down on her roller-coaster seat, locking her in place. She felt the thrill of excitement humming in her chest, mixed with that spark of desperation to jump out and run.

Arden leaned her head back and closed her eyes, a small smile playing on her lips.

"I almost forgot what it's like to be warm."

"We were only outside for an hour."

"But a long, cold hour."

"Sorry, it was miserable for you."

"It was nice actually, but I'll still let you make it up to me. Tokens are on you." Arden opened her eyes and turned her head, not bothering to lift it from the seatback. There was something intimate about that lazy turn, her dark hair spilling across the white of the seat like she was lying in bed.

Focus. "I think I can swing a few tokens."

Arden took her in, trailing her eyes up and down Reese. "Why are you squished like that? Here." She slid over a bit and patted the small middle seat next to her.

Reese felt the rollercoaster clicking upwards as she unstuck her legs, feeling the ghost of the position in her knees as she moved toward Arden.

The driver threw an arm behind the headrest of the passenger's seat, lowering his sunglasses and taking them in.

"Hello ladies, where are we headed?"

His shellacked hair gleamed even in the low light of the car. The air in the car was thick with what cologne companies thought rugged mountains smell like.

"You should have the address in the app, right?" Arden asked with a tight smile.

"Right, just making sure you weren't in for a change of plans."

Arden shook her head, and the silence stretched out. They should have just walked the few miles to the arcade. She could have given Arden her coat.

The car lurched away from the curb, and Reese's stomach hit her throat.

Their thighs brushed, and Reese was acutely aware of each place their bodies touched. Every curve their daredevil driver screeched through tossed them together.

Arden gripped Reese's knee, holding on for dear life.

"Are you ok?" Her voice was loud next to Reese's ear, but it barely rose above the bass rattling the windows next to them.

"I'm ok this is just a little—" The drive was scary but it was Arden's hand on her leg that had her heart in her throat.

The driver accelerated through a turn. Reese let out a yelp and threaded her arm through Arden's. The seatbelt in the back was doing very little to hold her in place.

The car bottomed out over a speedbump and the driver swore and came to an abrupt stop as the engine sputtered. "Must have flooded it."

The car made terrible noises as he tried to get it going again, but Reese was grateful for the reprieve from his driving.

The music continued to jackhammer.

The drive continued for a few more blocks in a cycle of peeling out, collecting speed, and then violent shifts that often ended with the car stalling.

The third time the car stalled out, Reese thought for sure she was going to be sick. She slumped back against the seat and closed her eyes as the driver swore at the car. Next to her, Arden wore a look of annoyance she'd been familiar with from their very first meeting.

The car sounded like a fork in a garbage disposal.

Arden reached forward and tapped the driver's shoulder, signaling for him to unlock the door.

"We'll just get out here."

"But we're still a few blocks from your destination. I've almost got it started."

"That's ok, really." Arden shoved the passenger's seat forward and opened the door with her foot. She gingerly climbed out and reached a hand back to help Reese.

Reese fell out of the car laughing—her ears ringing from the bass.

The driver rolled the window down.

"Ladies, please wait. I just need a minute, and I'll get it working again. I swear this has never happened to me before."

"Have a good day," Arden said as the driver got the car started and sped away the length of a football field before stalling again. Setting off a new fit of laughter.

As they caught their breath, Arden linked their arms together and led a woozy Reese away from the curb. "Is it just me or do you get the feeling that's something he says quite a bit?"

"Oh definitely. I assume that is always what happens. Hey, thanks so much for getting me to try something new." Reese rolled her eyes but followed up with a smile.

"We're just getting started."

BEST SHOT PENNY'S was perfect: old, run down, and deserted. Beneath her feet, little puffs of dust rose from the sawdust covering the floor. The neon glow of pinball machines and their tinny music called to her. Reese would not be surprised if she had died on that boardwalk and been driven straight to heaven in the back of an aggressively air-freshened muscle car.

"Hold out your hands." Arden reappeared beside her and gave her a mischievous smile.

Reese cupped her hands in front of her. "Wait, I was supposed to get these."

"I feel like I need to make up for the terrible ride I talked you into."

Arden poured a handful of brass tokens into Reese's palms. The rush of possibility hit her—a day to do only what she wanted and not worry about anything else. She couldn't remember the last time she'd had a day like that. Her real-world worries vanished from her like pellets of Pac-Man lost in a maze of ghosts. The only currency that mattered here had no cash value.

They took their places at games next to each other and played their hearts out in silence interrupted only by trash talk. It was a strange thing for Reese to feel content next to another person. In all her months alone, she hadn't missed company. She hadn't wanted that unpredictable chaos of sharing a space with someone. In fact, she hadn't missed anything except for those times when she could hear Judith singing opera through the walls and longed for a bone-deep silence.

But stealing glances at Arden in the dusty arcade made her feel sad for herself in a way she'd never stopped to do before. Arden leaned forward over a pinball machine. Her brow furrowed in concentration and her hair falling forward as the flashing neon lights played across her face. She looked like an 80s music video, only missing the fingerless gloves.

Reese gripped the sides of her own game until the metal edges dug clean lines into her palms, just to keep herself from reaching forward and tucking a rogue strand of hair back behind Arden's ear. She couldn't remember ever feeling an impulse like that. Sure, she'd had her fair share of nights holding back Lo's hair when she was sick, but there was an undercurrent of obligation there. This was something else. A tenderness she didn't recognize and wasn't sure she liked.

She'd be fine. Reese just needed to keep reminding herself that this day was an anomaly.

TEN

The sun was slipping behind the buildings when they made their trek toward the subway. They were both feeling done with cars for the foreseeable future. On the east coast, the sun set before 5 pm like an employee sneaking out of the office and hoping no one notices.

A full, perfect day. That was how long Reese had spent with Arden and not once did she want her to disappear. Reese wasn't sure how to feel about that. She knew how she *should* feel. She knew how she *expected* to feel: exhausted. Ready to put white noise on her stereo headphones and be alone for three days.

But as their shoulders collided on the train, that wasn't how she felt at all. She wasn't sure what to make of this energy flickering through her like buzzy overhead light.

What she felt instead was unsettled and unpredictable. Nervous energy coursed through her; the kind of electricity that made it hard to stand still. She wanted to dance, and the thought horrified her. She was not a person who danced. She was not a person who liked spending time with other people. She was perfectly happy alone. Or at least solidly content.

She needed Arden to do her a favor and be annoying. Maybe she could correct Reese's grammar or pronunciation and free her from whatever the hell these feelings were.

Reese wanted to be able to enjoy her night alone in peace, instead of whatever this empty feeling in her stomach was. Annoyance was so much easier to understand. Cleaner. Instead all she wanted to do was reach out and touch Arden, she wanted to stay on the gross, noisy subway all night if it kept this day with her from ending.

Getting close to people always made everything messy. Decisions got blurred. It was like waking up and trying to do things before she put on her glasses. She was always so sure she could walk to the kitchen but more often than not she'd trip and fall into the wall. This, right now, felt like the moment right after her foot caught on the rug, but before her shoulder smacked into the unforgiving doorframe. All she could do was put her hands out to lessen the fall. But that embarrassing crash? It was inevitable.

Each time the train took a curve at an inadvisable speed her shoulder bumped into Arden's and Reese felt sparks. It was like she kept touching the third rail: inadvisable and irresistible. It made her want a million fast curves and trains stuck in tunnels for an indeterminate amount of time.

She sifted through her mind for ways to keep the date going like she was panning for gold but only finding rocks. Maybe they could walk some more? Or read next to each other? How did people spend time together? Were drinks still a thing?

The date was going so well. No, not a date. The day. The casual hangout with a colleague whose mouth Reese couldn't stop staring at. Who she wanted to kiss despite this disgustingly public setting, teeming with sneezing commuters and creepy men sitting with their legs so wide they seemed to straddle invisible horses.

In her defense, Arden put on lip balm like 20 times an hour, so it would have been weird *not* to look at her mouth. Disrespectful, really. Like going to a gallery and only looking at the floor.

The subway car creaked like one of those old wooden roller coasters meant to make you feel like a miner; your life endangered by poor structural integrity. You know, fun. They rattled around another hairpin turn and screeched into a station. The lights flickered and she felt like she was headed down to the depths of the earth.

The doors opened and in came a rush of violin music and about 1,000 people. She took a half step closer to Arden, angling her body towards hers.

Their forced proximity was charged. Reese didn't flinch when something unexpected brushed against her. Maybe she could handle being out in the world more than she'd thought. She wasn't hyperventilating in the warm crush of bodies on the packed car. The only thing currently making her breath come short was the way Arden kept parting her lips as though to say something and then deciding against it. Reese was thinking of ways to stay on the train all night next to Arden, their arms softly brushing from shoulder to fingertips like they were lying in bed. *She was in major trouble.*

"What are you smiling about?"

Arden's voice was soft, but it cut through the cacophony of the city. Reese could hear her as clearly as if she was listening over headphones in the studio. That was twice today that Reese was so tuned in to her that the rest of the noise just fell away. *I'm thinking about you.*

"Oh, just thinking about how badly I beat you at Pac-Man again. It's like you purposefully let the ghost catch you."

"What can I say? I've always wondered what it would be like to be haunted."

Reese laughed. "You know, you're weirder than I gave you credit for."

"I feel like I've been running up quite the tab. Annoying you with all of my helpful suggestions and revised lunch orders."

"To be fair, I've also been a little intense."

Arden squinted one eye and held her thumb and index finger a few millimeters apart.

"Ok, fine, more than a little, but in my defense, I don't really like people."

"You know that's not really a defense, right?"

"I have gotten that feedback."

The speaker crackled to life and the conductor said something garbled and unintelligible as the train pulled into the station. Train announcements were a very specific regional dialect.

"Well this is me." Arden took a step toward the doors as they whooshed open. "If you stay on for two more stops, you'll be right by your hotel."

Arden hopped off the train with a small wave and Reese felt like the door was closing on more than just the day, but a chance she would never get back if she wasn't brave.

Reese elbowed the people streaming on out of the way and slipped through the sliding doors right before they guillotined closed.

"Arden, wait." Her own voice was higher than she'd ever heard it, something buoyant in it, not quite desperation. Was this hope? She'd have to remember this combination for future books.

Several people turned to look at her. She felt like an actress on a stage and it made her want to jump onto the empty tracks to escape.

But then Arden turned, and all the noise stopped. Her dark hair fell over her shoulder in a wave. How did anyone look so beautiful in a subway station?

"Did I forget something?" Arden drew her brows together, the right side of her mouth curving upward. That absolutely unfair dimple on full display.

"No, I did." Reese's heart was in her throat.

Reese took a step forward and then another.

The worst thing that can happen is you ruin everything. And for the first time in forever the risk felt worth it. She felt worth it.

"What did you forget?"

Arden's eyes dropped to her lips. As she started to lean forward, an annoyed business bro bumped her shoulder from behind and sent her crashing into Arden who caught her. *Of course, she did. This entire day is like some alternate Disney reality where good things happen.*

"Are you ok?"

"I'm..." Reese didn't finish her thought, instead she turned off her brain and closed the gap between them.

Arden's mouth was soft beneath hers for the briefest of moments before she broke the contact. Arden had only taken one step back, but Reese felt the space between them stretching like a canyon.

"What's wrong?" Reese took in the startled look on Arden's face like a punch to the stomach. How had she misread this? It was so rare that she liked someone and she felt that with Arden. Reese thought the day had been perfect for her, too. But it was possible all Arden wanted from her was friendship. *Or, more horrifying, maybe all she wanted was for Reese to do the job she'd been hired to do.*

Arden pulled her phone from her pocket and glanced at the display. "I'm sorry, I can't, I'm late for a thing. I—I'm sorry." Arden spun and stepped into the crowd streaming around them, Reese lost track of her immediately.

"And that's why trying's not worth it. My plants would never ditch me in a grungy subway station." Reese trudged down the city street, stepping around the puddles of snowmelt from the sunny day.

"That's the lesson you're taking away?" Lo's voice sounded somewhere between amused and exasperated. "And where are you? It's never a good idea for you to walk angry."

"I'm not walking angry, I'm walking embarrassed. There's a difference. I put myself out there and now I wish I hadn't. I wish I was still in Chicago with Judith annoying me."

"No, you don't. Speaking of Judith, have you been ignoring her calls?"

"Wait how do you—" She heard a plunk like a stone dropping into a well as the cold water seeped into her boot. Runoff from a city snow melt? She should probably just head straight to the emergency room. For the first time all day she felt truly cold.

"Did I lose you?"

"No, I stepped in a puddle and now I have hypothermia."

"Ok, Jack Dawson. Find a floating door, you'll be fine."

"What were you saying about Judith?"

"She just called me the other day. We had a nice chat."

"How did she get your number?"

"I assumed she got it from you."

"She must have found it in my apartment. Her invasiveness is an art form. She must have gotten it from the emergency numbers on my fridge. Was there a succulent emergency? Too much water, not enough?"

"I think she's just worried about you. She's used to seeing you every day and she said you haven't been returning her calls or texts."

"She's watching my plants because *she* insisted. Sue me if I don't think we need to talk every day."

"You could be a little nicer. She's a sweet lady. Once I'm out of this joint, she's going to teach me to play canasta."

"You could be a little less on everyone's side but mine."

"I'm always on your side, Reesey. That doesn't mean agreeing with everything you do or say. Call Judith. And don't cancel your museum plans just because she had to go. You don't know what she has going on. And she did drop everything and spend the day losing to you in video games."

"And she didn't complain," Reese mumbled.

"What was that?"

"She didn't complain—she wasn't a sore loser."

"Great. So, don't be a sore winner, dude. See how things go on your creepy date. You can't just write off a woman willing to go to a graveyard with you as a fun event. That's something... special."

"I've been meaning to ask how everything's going there —how are you feeling?"

"Oh, you know, same as last time and the time before that. The food's pretty good here though."

"That's not really what I meant, Lo."

On the other end of the line, Reese heard someone calling to Lo and then Lo's voice muffled, probably because she'd lowered the phone so she could yell back. "Look, sweet baby R, I've gotta go. I've got an hour for game night and my partner's getting antsy."

"Fine, go, Yahtzee your heart out."

"I always do. Call Judith."

REESE HAD BEATEN the sun out of bed by several hours. She'd spent the night brooding. Tossing and turning in the luxurious and infuriating hotel bed. The kind of night where she knew she'd drifted off at some point, even if she felt like she hadn't. Wondering if she should be easier on Arden and deciding no; only to start the whole consideration cycle over again. Maybe Lo was right and she'd misunderstood Arden walking away from her. Though could someone backing away from a kiss and fleeing really be misinterpreted?

Lo had also gotten into her head about Judith, too. So much so that Reese had sent her a quick text, a gif of a dancing cactus around three am and was shocked to get an immediate response. Judith had sent her six hearts and a rainbow. She'd always pegged Judith as the kind of person who was in bed by nine so she could be up with the sun to get in a full day of meddling. But Reese had to admit, in the daily pictures Judith sent her plants looked happier than they had in months. Maybe she could find the mental fortitude to call her later.

She searched for places to get the best flat white in Brooklyn as she shimmied into her jeans. One benefit of

New York at dawn was the streets emptied of people. Its usual chaos subdued like a sleeping toddler.

Reese slipped into a thick wool sweater and her leather jacket. In typical March fashion, the warmth of yesterday was a distant memory and the sky looked gray and mean, even with the sun rising.

She grabbed her phone and opened the door. The first thing she felt was warm liquid seeping through her wool sweater. The smell of espresso greeted her with a slight undertone of hay. Wool was not made to get wet.

Arden blinked back at her looking like she'd just accidentally pulled the fire alarm.

"You've got to be kidding me. Is this like your signature move?" Reese pulled the wet sweater away from her body.

"You know what they say: no good deed..."

"But why am I always the one being punished?"

"Funny, last time it felt like we were in it together. Here, let me help you." Arden reached forward and pressed a napkin to Reese's chest.

Reese's breath knotted below her palm. She needed to get past this infatuation. Arden had been clear yesterday. So brutally clear. They were colleagues and temporary colleagues at that.

Reese placed her hand over Arden's and felt it still. She grabbed it gently and pulled it away from her chest. "What are you doing here?"

"I was bringing you coffee because I wanted to talk about yesterday."

Oh god. Was Arden about to lecture her about appropriate boundaries and how all that mattered to her was the deadline? If she'd brought a coffee to soften the blow of whatever she came here to say it couldn't be good. Reese had to shut that down before it started. "There's nothing to talk about. We had a nice day before I ruined it. I'm embarrassed and I'm sorry. Can we please just move on?"

"No, don't be like that. I promise it won't kill us to talk about it."

What was with people wanting to talk about things? Had no one ever heard of avoiding things forever? Just find a cozy apartment and insulate yourself from reality like an emotional bubble wrap?

"Fine. Come in, I guess." Reese took a step back into the room and held the door open. Glad she'd had endless amounts of time that morning to stress clean.

"Were you on your way out?"

"I was going to get coffee, but I suppose I can try wringing some out of my sweater. Thanks for bringing it by the way."

"Sorry for spilling it on you. Again. This was not my devious way to get you out of your shirt."

"Oh trust me, I in no way think you're trying to do that." Reese dug through her bag and pulled out a clean shirt before heading to the bathroom.

Arden moved as though to follow her before stopping short.

"I just need a minute and then we can talk."

Arden nodded once as Reese closed and locked the bathroom door.

She stripped off her sweater and slumped against the door. Arden being here wanting to talk and bringing coffee as a bribe, albeit one that had left an angry red streak across Reese's stomach, could not be a good sign. But the thought of Arden in her hotel room sent a flutter of anticipation through her.

She touched the sore skin on her ribs and was met with the wet fabric of her bra. Perfect. Could she pull on a shirt and face Arden braless? Probably not the smartest move for someone so recently rejected. It was desperate even if it was circumstantial. And Reese was never desperate. She didn't need anything from Arden besides the money from this job.

Reese sighed into the empty bathroom and the tile bounced it back to her like she was inside a shell. She knew what she had to do and no part of her wanted to do it. She would rather let Judith go through her dresser and fly out with a bra but she'd tossed her phone on the bed.

"Arden?" Reese said through the cracked door.

Silence.

"Arden?" This time Reese raised her voice beyond a whisper, trying to inject the confidence of a character who had her life together.

"Yeah?"

"I forgot to grab a bra and this one's soaked, would you mind grabbing one from my bag?"

"You, um, want me to go through your bag?"

"Want is a pretty strong word."

"Right, of course. I can do that. Are you ok? Are you burned? Do you want me to go see if the front desk has antibiotic cream?"

"No, just going through my underwear and grabbing a bra will be sufficiently horrifying, thanks."

"I'm so sorry. I found this place that is supposed to have the best flat whites because David said that's your favorite and then once again, I totally ruined it by dumping it all over you."

"You went to The Creamery?"

"How did you—"

"Seems like we did the same google search this morning."

Reese eased the door shut again—she should probably

watch Arden go through her stuff but she wasn't a masochist. She'd always subscribed to the school of what-I-don't-know-can't-hurt-me.

What a way for a beautiful woman to see her underwear. That could have happened in so many different ways. She had *imagined* that happening so many different ways like—

The knock on the door was right next to her ear and Reese ducked even though she should have been expecting it. She cracked the door and a second later a red lace bra dangled through the gap. By far the sexiest one in her luggage. A choice she would now have to spend the day not obsessing over.

ELEVEN

The bra was a little uncomfortable, that's why she could feel it acutely on their walk to The Creamery and not because Arden had handed it to her, had selected it, *knew* she was wearing it. Nope, definitely didn't have anything to do with that.

"Are you ok?" Arden set down a white ceramic mug in front of her, a thin layer of foam on its surface.

"Yeah, yup, definitely. Everything's fine. Why do you ask?" Reese wrapped her hands around the mug to have something to do with them but withdrew them immediately as the hot mug burned her fingers. *What was with this day? Coffee is not supposed to be the enemy.*

"It's just... nothing. I wanted to talk to you about something, not try to make you share things with me."

"Ok, should I be nervous? Did I lose the job?"

"What? No, it's nothing like. You're doing great, even if you do get a bit twangy unexpectedly." Arden's eyes twinkled

"I do no such thing," Reese drawled in her best old western.

"Thanks for showing me it's not as bad as it could be." Arden laughed.

Reese pointed a finger at Arden. "Hey, I'm at this fancy coffee shop at an ungodly hour of my own free will. How about we save criticisms of my voice for the end?"

The coffee shop was mostly deserted, not much call for early coffee on the weekends. It was quaint, with little mismatched tables dotting the floor. Nothing like the intimidating café of the salad incident. Reese was grateful for the open tables around them and the acoustic music coming from the speakers. It was just the right amount of noise. She felt comfortable enough to have a conversation without being overheard but she wasn't overwhelmed by the crush of noise most places usually carry.

Maybe she should try finding a coffee shop like this back home. It would be nice to have someone else make her coffee sometime.

Arden shifted in her chair like the legs were uneven and she couldn't find her balance.

"I appreciate you coming. Even though you're only here because I unexpectedly showed up at your hotel room and ruined your morning and your outfit. I'm so sorry about that by the way I just—"

"It's probably better to just say what you need to say. I mean you can apologize to me all day, both for spilling coffee on my favorite sweater and for selecting a bra that was sure to show through this white shirt I'm wearing." Arden's face went as red as Reese's bra and she felt a little smug about it. She maturely took a sip of her coffee to keep from gloating. "And I suppose I can apologize all day for putting you in an awkward situation yesterday. Maybe we just call a truce and go back to being colleagues."

"No, that's not what I—look I'm a little nervous. I haven't said this to many people who aren't like...me."

Reese could feel the anxiousness rolling off of Arden like fog. She was picking at one of her nails, chipping the black polish off like she was sculpting marble. There was something in the gesture that cracked Reese's heart. She wasn't sure she could handle Arden being vulnerable if she didn't want to fall for her.

She didn't realize she'd reached for Arden's hand until she felt Arden's fingers tense beneath hers before relaxing. Arden flipped her palm up and wove their fingers together.

"Thanks, I wasn't expecting it to be this hard. It's much easier to say in a basement full of twenty strangers."

The pieces clicked into place like the last pin in a lock she'd been picking. Should she put her out of her misery? Something about the way Arden's shoulders were creeping up near her ears stopped Reese from letting her know that she knew.

It seemed important for Arden to get this out and she could give her a safe place to land. A good experience. She knew from her sister's horror stories how critical that could be.

"I'm sober. Thirteen months. That's where I had to go yesterday. I've been having trouble getting to meetings with the time in the studio and writing. Plus, Sophia, my agent, seems to dislike them. I'm not sure why I told you that last part."

She felt Arden's hand tighten its grip on hers. "You can exhale now."

She heard the whooshing sound of Arden's breath.

"I think it's great that you're sober. Thirteen months is incredible. It's not the same but my sister Lo is sober too. Well, she's getting there again."

"I didn't know you had a sister."

"I do. Do you want to talk about it? Should I ask questions? Not ask questions?"

"Well, yesterday I had a perfect day. Which honestly surprised me. I thought we'd fight the whole time. And I felt bad running off like that, but I really needed to check in before making any decisions. Even if I really wanted to kiss you back."

Reese blinked at Arden. Was it possible that she was still at her hotel in a restless sleep?

"Was that the wrong thing to say?" Arden withdrew her hand from Reese's like sliding a plate out of a stack. "I know you might not feel the same as you did yesterday, knowing this."

"That wasn't the wrong thing to say. And I'm not put off by it. It's a big deal only in that it's a huge accomplishment that should be celebrated. I'm just surprised by your honesty, I guess."

"Honesty is pretty fundamental to me."

"Also, I was asking if you wanted to talk about why you got sober. I wasn't trying to get you to confess to anything about yesterday. Although, I'm not sorry that you did."

"There's not much to tell. Or there is and I still haven't quite figured out how to tell it. I had a novel, *Something Sweet,* that did really well—it was about these rival pastry chefs in Baltimore near the height of the Great British Baking Show taking off in America."

"Oh, I think I've heard of that one!"

"Heard of but not read?" Arden raised an eyebrow.

"Let's not get into those details," Reese vowed to focus on listening.

"Anyway, the book got optioned and I went to LA to work on the screenplay. I figured it would be easy—I'm a writer, I wrote the book. If anything, a script should be easier—some dialogue and stage directions. I was about as naive as people who assume anyone can write a romance because it uses tropes and always has a happy ending.

"It was hard, and it was lonely, and I felt very bad at what I was doing. I didn't have any friends in LA, but I did realize that working in bars with a drink made me feel less lonely and took the sharp edge off my doubt. But it also made the pages I turned in worse."

Arden was speaking so fast that some parts were hard to understand but Reese got the gist. And she didn't dare interrupt. Telling this story seemed to be releasing some pressure Arden had been carrying around inside her. She gave Arden a reassuring smile, even though she seemed to be focused on some point over Reese's shoulder. Probably for the same reason Lo hated making amends.

"The production team got annoyed when I missed one deadline and then another. They brought in this male author to write the story and he just... ruined it. And they loved it. They just fawned all over this guy. I had failed at this huge opportunity and here was some smug guy getting all the credit for my story.

"They called me to come in and sign off on the script. I had a few drinks before to take the edge off, but I lost track and it was more than a few. I crashed my car into the other writer's parked car—cops came, the whole bit.

"New York's not easy but LA is a different beast entirely. Sophia came out to visit and had me in rehab the next day. This book, the one you're narrating will be my first since that project fell apart. I get the feeling Sophia had to move hell and high water to get my publisher to not drop me."

So many pieces of Arden were shifting to fit together in

Reese's mind. Her single-minded intensity to get this book right. Even the way she had trouble standing up to her evil agent made more sense now. That kind of act probably created a huge feeling of obligation. She made a mental note to check in with Lo. She'd never want her to feel like she owed her anything.

"Thanks for telling me that—you definitely didn't have to. I still don't understand why you're putting so much pressure on yourself with this book. Plus the book is *good.*"

"Well, I just disappeared from the writing world and people have been speculating why. There are some really good theories out there. My favorite one is that I had a secret baby."

"For what it's worth, they'd be stupid to drop you. Don't your books always make the bestsellers list?"

"I think you underestimate the risk they see when they look at me. Which is ironic since I am so much less risky now than when I was drinking heavily while writing. Now I'm clean enough to sell Girl Scout cookies. Who doesn't like those?"

"Are they made with real girl scouts?"

"Addams Family—I love that movie." Arden sat back in her chair and smiled. She took the first sip of her drink, which Reese realized was actually tea, and grimaced. It was probably cold by now. Reese took a sip of her own long-forgotten drink and confirmed her theory.

"Me too, it's the perfect amount of nostalgic and creepy."

"I mean it's got some racist moments too. I remember Wednesday in a headdress at camp."

"You're right. So many movies I loved as a kid have issues like that."

"I know you weren't asking about yesterday, but I would like to talk about it."

"I'm really sorry I put you in that position. I didn't know you were sober." Reese felt like even more of a jerk now that Arden had shared with her. She'd respect whatever Arden wanted and she'd work double-time to make sure this book was as perfect as it could be; read by someone who allegedly mispronounces common words like 'and' and 'Sarah'.

"It's fine, don't worry about that. I wasn't rejecting you. It's just that—" Arden paused, looking down at her hands around her cup. Her nerves seemed to be gathering again like storm clouds. Her knuckles were ghostly against the white porcelain mug.

"You need to focus on your sobriety. I totally get that, and I respect it."

"No, well, I mean, yes, I do but that's not why—"

"Plus, we work together."

"No, can you just let me finish? Wait, is that a problem for you—us working together? It's not for much longer."

"Obviously not a big enough one based on yesterday."

"I just didn't feel right without you knowing that I'm in recovery. It's a big decision and I didn't want you to feel like you had to act like it was nothing. I kind of hate when people do that, to be honest. It's not nothing. Getting sober almost killed me. And it shapes everything I do. But I needed to check in with myself before telling you all of that. I wanted to be centered first before I..." she trailed off, sitting up a little taller as her gaze dropped to Reese's mouth.

"Before you what?"

"Before I did this." Arden half rose from her chair and leaned across the table. Her dark eyes searched Reese's for a moment before she slid one hand along her jaw. Reese felt the warm touch on her face, and she leaned forward to close the gap between them.

Arden's mouth was soft and warm beneath hers. The table dug into her hips but that didn't stop her from leaning forward more and wrapping a hand behind Arden's neck, fingers curling into the silky dark hair.

She could taste the tea on Arden's lips as she deepened the kiss, something sweet and slightly floral. She'd consider liking tea if she could always have it like this.

Reese's head spun as she felt the vibration of Arden's moan against her mouth. She smiled into the kiss before pulling back slightly to rest her forehead against Arden's. Reese had forgotten they were in a public place, an oversight she never could have imagined having a week ago.

"I really, really wish you had told me yesterday. I can't believe I spent an entire day not knowing what kissing you felt like."

"It's not always so easy. And I didn't want you to think less of me. Or get scared. Or start treating me like I'm some fragile person."

"I wouldn't."

"You know how some people treat coming out as a one-time event. Like you tell your family you're queer and you're done. Like somehow the rest of the world just gets an email notice about it or something?"

"Right, except coming out never ends. You make a decision whether or not to do it again every time you meet someone."

"Yeah, and you're always doing these calculations. Like when's the right time to come out. How should I do it? Casually mention a girlfriend or an ex? Or confrontationally in response to an insulting comment? Or talk about some horrible new thing the president's doing or a hate crime?"

"I don't interact with people much, but I take your point."

"Telling people I'm sober feels like that. It's like coming out over and over basically every time I'm at a restaurant or a bar or someone's house or concert or any sort of professional function or wedding. It's coming out as sober over and over and it can be exhausting. Because there's so much judgment tied to it and curiosity. Everyone wants the rock bottom story. It's like a car crash on the expressway—people love to stare while pretending to be concerned.

"Sure, some people are supportive, but some feel pity, or just don't get it. Some people think I'm pregnant and then I have to clarify even more. And some people, including people I care about, are really dismissive. Dismissive is the worst. When people think it's a phase. Because that's my biggest fear. Messing up. Falling back into it. Undoing everything I've done.

"That's a really long way of saying I wanted to tell you earlier, but I wanted to be prepared for your response, whatever it was going to be. And I didn't want to kiss you without telling you because it feels wrong."

TWELVE

Reese pulled her collar up to block the sharp bite of the wind. The sky was overcast and a perfect day for a graveyard date. The weather was creating ambiance better than any candle lit dinner. *Shit. Should she have planned dinner? Was this a date? Should she text to clarify? No, she kissed you yesterday. It's a date.*

She was pretty sure her phone had stopped updating the time ever since she left her hotel to meet Arden. She'd gotten there a little early. Ok, a lot early. And had mostly been doing her best to stay out of the wind.

Arden had said to meet her by the gates that 'look like they belong on a medieval jail cell'. The metal next to her head ended in a jagged spike, so she was fairly confident she was in the right place. Reese leaned against the rusted iron gates that led into the cemetery as she waited, the cold of the air and metal seeping through her leather jacket as she read another write up about the pop-up museum.

"You look deep in thought. I thought we agreed no working today, just this." Arden pointed back and forth between them.

Her voice was like a campfire, bright and warm. Reese took a step closer. Just seeing Arden made Reese forget how cold and stiff and bordering on annoyed she was. Arden wore a dark gray wool coat and a black beanie that was somewhere between hipster and night watchman.

"I was reading about the skeletons on display. Did you know that the human hand has 54 bones?"

"Does it now?" Arden reached for Reese's hand and held it gently as though examining it. "It feels like yours are about to freeze. Shall we?" Arden entwined their fingers and led Reese through the gates.

"Oh, wait. Here." Reese reached into her bag. "I brought you something."

"What is it?"

"It's coffee."

"No, what is this?" Arden tapped her finger against the silver travel mug. "It looks like it's about to be launched into space."

"Well, it's supposed to be completely spill proof."

Arden's mouth dropped open in mock outrage but a smile claimed her face a moment later. "Wow, you're so subtle."

"Listen, I felt like I owed you a coffee but I need this outfit to make it through the day."

The museum was even better and creepier than Reese had imagined. She ran her fingers along rough granite gravestones that rose from the earth at odd angles like broken teeth. The skeletons she had wanted to see were laid out on the grass; arms crossed over their chests in eternal rest. Arden seemed just as into it as her, reciting all the macabre facts she'd absorbed on her previous visit.

She was acutely aware of Arden's arm tucked through hers as they wove their way through the yard.

"Have you ever considered writing a creepy book?"

"The one I'm working on now isn't creepy, but one of the main characters loves vampires and hosts a podcast about them called Love Bites, which she also uses to dole out advice."

Reese laughed. "That sounds like my kind of romance novel."

"Maybe I can drag you back to New York to record it when it's ready."

She knew Arden was going for sweet, but the underlying truth of her statement was like dirt on top of a casket. This was temporary. Even if it was good, it wasn't going anywhere. Arden was already thinking ahead to when it was over. She'd just make the most of it—it was a fun distraction while she was here, not real life.

"Where did you go just now?"

"Nowhere. Let's go see the brains." Reese pulled on Arden's arm, leading her to the far side of the cemetery.

THEY WERE NEARING the end of the exhibits, and Reese felt satisfied she'd seen enough oddities for the day. Every time she looked at Arden, dark eyes were watching her in return. And the heat of Arden's gaze on her was enough to keep her warm.

"You're watching me."

"Yes."

"Why?"

"Because I'm trying to decide if it would be disrespectful to kiss you here."

"Let's leave. I don't think either of us needs to be haunted."

"You're right, we've already got that covered."

They walked through the gates and Arden backed her up against the stone wall. "Are we in the clear?"

Arden's dark eyes were so beautiful as they searched hers. The sky dimmed around them like a scarf had been thrown over a lamp. The light playing across Arden's full lips was gentle.

Reese reached out and ran her thumb along Arden's lower lip. "Perfect. This is perfect." She grabbed the lapels of Arden's coat and the wool felt soft beneath her fingers. She pulled Arden toward her to close the distance between them and Arden laughed and braced an arm against the wall next to Reese's head. She knew it was partially for balance, but it also had a James Dean level of sexy to it.

"You should kiss me now. The ghosts won't mind."

Arden's cold hands framed Reese's face as she kissed her deeply. It wasn't the soft kiss of the coffee shop. There was a hunger behind it as Arden gently bit Reese's bottom lip and stepped closer, pressing Reese's back against the stone wall. Reese felt the flame of Arden's kiss everywhere; standing there pressed against the cold stone in the sharp wind was the warmest she'd felt all day.

Their breaths came in sharp gasps as they broke apart. The ethereal clouds of their breath rising like smoke between them.

"So what now?" Reese leaned her forehead against Arden's. She could have kissed her like that, out here in the cold against this abrasive stone wall for hours, days.

"How about dinner?"

"Um," Reese paused to buy time. She wanted to keep spending time with Arden but the thought of continuing to be around people exhausted her. Reese's heart sank a bit, but she tried not to show it. If going out was important, she could do it.

"Hey, what are you thinking in there?" Arden tapped her forehead gently.

"What? Nothing." Had anyone ever paid this much attention? Listened so deeply to her silence? Cared enough to push for more?

"That's a very tortured nothing, but I'll let you use your free pass. So the sushi place I'm thinking of is right near my apartment. It's popular but we can probably get a table."

Waiting in line to sit in a crowded room of people made Reese feel very tired. What she wanted was to be alone. But the thought of going back to recharge in her hotel room wasn't the comfort she expected it to be. What she wanted was to be alone with Arden. Why didn't that thought unsettle her? She usually couldn't wait to be alone, truly phone-off-shades-drawn-noise-cancelling-headphones-on alone. Even with her occasional one-night stands she was rushing those women out in the morning, pressing a granola bar and a to-go coffee mug into their hands that she assured them they didn't need to return.

So why did the thought of time with Arden ending feel like the last few slow songs at a school dance? Like the last opportunity to make the night magic was about to pass her by? Surely she could be as brave as a middle schooler making a move under the pink strobe lights.

"I'll take your silence to the dinner question as a definite maybe? If you're too tired, I'd also be happy to walk you back to your hotel."

Reese felt like she was on the edge of something. She could either back away to the safety of her hotel and bolt the door, or she could jump into the unknown.

"I haven't had sushi in a long time. Chicago might be right on the water, but lake fish does not good sushi make."

"Excellent—the wait for a table shouldn't be too bad, but I can call ahead and put our names in."

THE RELIEF REESE felt when they approached the restaurant and it was closed for a private event made her weak. She'd been pushing her exhaustion and anxiety down their entire walk over.

"Ok, change of plans. I can try looking up other places. What do you like to eat?"

"I'm going to suggest something, and I don't want you to read too much into it. But would it be possible to get takeout and eat at your place? Maybe from that food cart over there? Not to just invite myself over, but I kind of hit my max of being out in the world at seven this morning and have been running on social fumes ever since."

"What were you doing out at seven in the morning?" Arden paused, shaking her head, "I recognize that that wasn't the most relevant part of your sentence. Yes, dinner at my place sounds perfect to me—we can make it like a picnic."

THIRTEEN

Reese wasn't sure what she expected Arden's place to look like, but it definitely wasn't what the door had just swung open onto. The studio apartment was meticulously clean, the wooden floors glossy and the surfaces clear. Two walls were painted a lush deep teal that reminded Reese of the ocean. It was as pristine as her own apartment, assuming Judith hadn't used it for canasta night.

"Your place is nice."

"You sound surprised."

"Aren't writers supposed to be messy? I have some idea of chaos and creativity going together."

Even the desk had only a laptop and a pinkish crystal lamp on it. No scraps of note paper or pens, or even cords. The only clutter, if you could call it that, were the plants that lined the far wall of the open studio space. They surrounded a floor to ceiling window that looked like something lifted from a church, thick glass panels bisected by black iron fittings.

The windows had beveled edges that bounced the streetlights outside back into the room like a prism.

Arden laughed. "I'm naturally pretty messy, but cleaning helps me focus, especially if I can't get to a meeting. Or if I'm avoiding writing an emotional scene. My friends from rehab say I replaced drinking with dusting, and they're not wrong." She gathered her hair into a messy bun and she suddenly looked so much like that night she showed up at Reese's hotel room.

Arden had turned away from her and headed to the open kitchen, which gave Reese a minute to scan the bookcase by the door. A lot of poetry and an early copy of East of Eden bound in blue cloth faded with years of sun. It was one of Reese's favorites.

"Do you want anything to drink? I have water: tap, filtered, and seltzer. If you're feeling fancy, I probably have a lime around here somewhere that I can cut into wedges."

"A seltzer would be great." She shoved her hands in her pockets, wishing for something to do, anything to keep busy. Being in Arden's apartment felt intimate in a way Arden coming to her hotel room or seeing her half naked as they changed into David's workout clothes didn't.

Arden handed her a stemless wine glass, little bursts of carbonation coming over the top like fireworks. She laid out the grey wool blanket she'd grabbed onto the floor next to the couch—it was shot through with a pattern of red and orange and yellow like a desert sunset.

"Well, cheers." Arden held her gaze and leaned in to clink their glasses together. Little bits of green flashed in her eyes that Reese had never noticed before. Reese took a long drink.

"Do you want dinner?" Reese asked, opening the bag of takeout on the coffee table. "I think we have everything we need to make that picnic." Why was she panic hosting? This wasn't even her apartment. It wasn't even her *state*.

"Not really."

"No?" Reese paused midway through pulling containers out of the bag.

"I think we'll need it more later." Arden came up behind Reese and placed a hand on her hip. Her fingers wove a delicate pattern over her stomach that Reese felt echoes of on the insides of her thighs. With her free hand, Arden reached around and took the container from Reese's hand, letting it drop to the floor.

"What if that spills?"

"Don't worry, I'll clean later."

"But the blanket—"

Reese's protest was replaced with a groan as Arden slid a finger beneath her chin and gently tipped her head back. She kissed a trail along her jaw. Reese longed for words to read rather than the inarticulate series of breathy noises she was currently composing. How vulnerable to be completely herself in this moment.

"Is this ok?" Arden's breath was warm on Reese's neck, but it still sent a shiver through her.

"Mmm, very."

"And this?" Arden placed her mouth where her breath had kissed Reese's neck a second earlier.

Reese leaned back, letting Arden's dark hair fall over her shoulder and tease at the collar of her shirt. The scent of vanilla hit her like something warm and sweet and familiar. "Also that."

"I had a nice day outside with you, but all that open air was a little restrictive."

Reese turned and placed her arms around Arden's neck. "And what was restrictive about it?"

"All of this, for one." Arden slowly ran a finger from the button of Reese's jeans up to the front clasp of her bra beneath her shirt.

Reese gasped.

"Still ok?"

Reese nodded and placed a kiss on Arden's lips. When she pulled away, her own mouth was sweet and minty from whichever lip gloss Arden had on.

Arden brought a thumb to Reese's lower lip before leaning in. "This color looks good on you."

"Look, Arden, I want this but are you sure you're—"

"You don't have to take care of me, Reese. This is fun. Let this be fun." Arden sank back onto the couch and pulled Reese on top of her.

She straddled Arden's lap but held herself up, still not able to let go completely. She didn't want to take advantage if Arden wasn't ready. Reese knew first-hand how delicate early sobriety could be, how fragile. But also how important those decisions were, that agency.

Arden's hands came to rest on her shoulders as she pulled her down gently. Reese felt the pressure of Arden's hips between her legs and let out a small moan.

"On second thought, if you want to take care of me, I have a few ideas." Arden's eyes flashed. Reese's breath caught and her hesitation untethered itself. The excitement and mischief glittering in Arden's eyes took away whatever worry had been holding Reese back. It set her free.

She laid her palm flat over Arden's collar bone and pushed her back against the couch. Her hands came to brace on either side of Arden's head. She gripped the back of the couch as she brought their mouths together and gently bit Arden's lower lip.

Arden leaned forward to deepen the kiss, but Reese

replaced her hand on her chest to hold her in place. "If you want me to take care of you, then I think you should let me."

She tugged at the hem of Arden's shirt and pulled it over her head, throwing it behind her. She jumped when something crashed to the floor—a wine glass?

"Sorry," Reese said as she kissed along her neck, feeling the warm expanse of Arden's naked stomach beneath her.

"Don't be, I miss when I had a reason to be messy."

She reached behind and unclasped Arden's bra, her hands replacing it as soon as the cups fell away. Arden arched into the touch and Reese felt the power of the reaction radiate through her. She wanted to touch Arden, wanted Arden to touch her, but she also wanted to make this part last for as long as possible. If this was just fun she wanted to make a day of it.

She leaned back and Arden's groan of protest turned into something deeper—a growl—as Reese removed her own shirt and tossed it aside. Arden brought her hands to Reese's hips to pull them back together, but Reese caught her wrists and pressed them toward the couch. "You're not very good at being taken care of, are you?"

The dimple that appeared on Arden's cheek when she laughed undid Reese. "Maybe not, but show me what you had in mind."

Reese pressed their bodies together as she claimed Arden's mouth and rocked her hips in time with their kiss. Every time Arden's hands came off the couch, she moved them back. Arden's hips bucked beneath her as Reese rolled her nipple between her thumb and index finger.

She ran the fingers of her other hand beneath the top of Arden's pants and watched as she threw her head back. When Reese caught her gaze again all of the green was gone from her eyes, her pupils blown.

Reese slid off the couch. Arden watched as she slid out of her pants, lips slightly parted. She sat forward, but Reese shook her head slowly and waited patiently for Arden to settle back before she continued. Whatever this little power play was it sent hot desire through her.

She slid Arden's jeans off her legs. The blanket felt soft beneath Reese's knees as she bit Arden's hip. Arden looped her thumb through the lace of her underwear.

"These, too." She tried to shift them down.

"We're getting there." Reese wove their fingers together as she brought her mouth down over the thin fabric. Arden broke free and tangled her hand in Reese's hair, her hips shifting forward.

"Ok, you can be the boss." Reese pulled the blue silk underwear down Arden's legs and ducked as she frantically kicked her legs free of them.

Reese pushed Arden's legs apart, running her hands up the insides of her thighs until they met at the apex. The wetness that met her there made her groan, and she leaned forward to trace her tongue through it.

Arden went still for a second, then her hand returned to Reese's hair, fingers weaving through her unruly curls.

She took her time exploring, running her tongue gently along every inch of Arden until she was squirming so much beneath her that precision became a challenge.

She brought her hands down the center of Arden's thighs, dipping into the wetness before drawing back and pushing Arden's legs further apart and draping them over her shoulders. Arden's hips lifted from the couch, but Reese was done guiding her back into place. She looped her arms around and grabbed Arden's hips, pulling her to her mouth.

She traced delicate circles on Arden's clit, increasing

the pressure the slightest amount each time Arden's thighs gripped around her.

"Reese, please." Arden's voice was low and desperate. "I need you to—"

Reese knew what she needed. She slipped one finger inside and then another. Tightening her other arm around Arden's hips, digging her nails into her thigh.

She kept her mouth on Arden, wishing she could see her, imagining her head thrown back. Dark hair cascading over the deep green of the couch. She wished she could watch it unfold, imprint it into her memory, but not enough to stop.

Arden's hand grasped Reese's hair, but not like she was trying to direct. It was like she needed something to hold on to. The sounds Arden was making were the sexiest that Reese had ever heard. Not light breathy moans but something deeper, more substantial, like something in her was breaking free.

Reese added a third finger, increasing her rhythm to the dance of Arden's hips until she went still beneath her. The hand in Reese's hair went slack and her scalp tingled. She leaned back to take in Arden's flushed face, head thrown back as though basking in the sun.

Arden's hand came down to still Reese's hand between her legs. "Just a minute, babe. And then we can go again."

FOURTEEN

The early morning light broke through the prisms of the floor-to-ceiling windows casting rainbows across the white comforter. The gayest windows in New York.

Arden's naked body stretched out on the surface of the bed, the white caps of the comforter rising around her. Her chest rose and fell gently like she was floating on a wave after a night of skinny dipping. Reese wanted to pull her back into the waters of the night before, feel the waves crash over them again and again. She settled for running a finger along the curve of her hip.

These past weeks had turned her life over. She couldn't remember the last time she'd woken in a bed that wasn't hers. Or slept next to someone. Not that she'd slept much, even once Arden finally passed out.

They'd made love for hours. No, that's not right. They'd had sex. Fun and great sex, but still just sex. She'd loved the moments when Arden finally lost control, but she'd also loved her directing.

A phone buzzed on the floor across the room, pulling

her thoughts back to the surface. The hardwood magnified the ringing to the volume of road work, a jackhammer demolishing her focus.

Reese rolled out of bed and scooped her pants up before the awful noise started again. From the pattern of the vibrations, she knew who it was. It helped that her sister was the only person who ever called her until recently, but she'd set Judith's alert to something equally obnoxious.

As she reached for the phone in her pocket, it buzzed again, wiggling from her grasp and onto the floor with a clatter. Like the phone didn't realize she was there to help.

She grabbed it quickly before it woke Arden, not that she seemed to be a light sleeper. Reese juggled the phone to her ear.

Reese cupped her hand around her mouth. "Hey, Lo. One second."

"What? Why are you whispering? I can barely hear you." Lo's voice came out of the speaker like a tyrant with a tiny megaphone. Earsplitting and distorted. Reese froze and held her breath.

Arden stirred lightly and turned onto her side, her back now to Reese. The gentle curve of her hip a perfect brushstroke in the gentle light. Her dark hair fanned out over the white sheets; Reese could still feel it silky between her fingers when Arden had gone down on her.

"Reese?"

Right. The phone.

"Just one second. I'm trying to—" She ducked slightly as the bathroom door creaked open like the noise was a water balloon she could narrowly avoid.

"Oh my god, you slept with her, didn't you? The writer lady? You're still there? I can't believe you spent the night!"

Reese pulled the bathroom door shut with a gentle

click. One thing she liked about her apartment was its walls. An embarrassment of them. Enough to divide every room.

"How do you do that?"

"I can hear it in your voice. You definitely got laid. You sound... happy."

"Gross. Cease and desist, Lo."

"Wait, where is she now?"

"Who?"

"You know exactly who."

"She's still asleep."

"Like naked in bed?"

Was there a way to drop her phone in the toilet and make it seem like an accident? Could she just never replace it and avoid all future conversations? Reese sank to the floor against the wall and pulled her knees to her chest to avoid the icy tile floor.

"I don't think sisters are supposed to ask about things like that."

"Things like you staying the night with someone for the first time in a million years? That's exactly the kind of things sisters are supposed to ask about."

"Ok, thank you, dear one, for taking an interest. She's not naked. There's a sheet."

"With all due respect, why the fuck did you answer your phone, Reesy? Go back to bed. Go get your girl. Everyone else can go to hell, which is essentially what voicemail is."

"Ok, she's not my girl, but I'll go."

"Wait, what was that shift in your voice. Do you want to leave? Are you ok?"

"No, that's the thing. I don't want to leave and I'm freaking out about it. Last night she said this was just fun, but I'm having feelings beyond fun."

"Ok, I know you don't do this much but that feeling? It's a good one. And sometimes it's fleeting, so go enjoy it. And call me later."

"Wait, why were you calling?"

"It's not important."

"It was 7-am-on-a-weekend important a few minutes ago when you decided to call."

"I need a place to crash for a bit. I wrapped up rehab. I was wondering if I could stay at your place."

"Of course. But I thought you were there through next week." Could people get out of rehab early? Or were the last few days like senior year where nothing really mattered anyway. How pissed would Lo be if she called Serenity Recovery and asked? Probably extremely.

Lo was silent for a moment on the other end of the line. Just the faintest hint of someone singing opera in the background. "Nope."

"You're already there, aren't you?"

"You have a naked woman in bed—why are we talking about this now? I'll call you later—actually, you call me, so I don't interrupt. Love you!"

The line went dead before Reese could respond. She made a mental note to call her later to talk about Judith.

Arden was still asleep when Reese slid back into the low bed. The sheet draped over her hip and she looked like a painting, almost sacred in the soft colorful light; like a stained-glass window people make pilgrimages to see. Her dark hair spread out over the pillow. She wanted to trace along the skin of Arden's back where the sheet had fallen down, but there was something so comforting in the shared silence. Instead, Reese watched the gentle rise and fall of her breathing as her eyes grew heavy.

It was full daylight when Reese opened her eyes, the kind of bright that felt personal with the way it stung her eyes. The sheets were a tangle next to her, but Arden was no longer held by them. She rolled over and looked to the kitchen before the gentle tapping of keys caught her attention.

Arden sat at her desk wrapped in a blanket, her head bent forward, headphones covering her ears. Reese lay frozen for a few minutes, enjoying watching her work but careful not to disturb her. Had she overstayed her welcome? Was this Arden's very nice way of saying she needed to work?

She wished she had woken up to Arden still in bed, but there was something very sexy about watching someone so focused on what they're doing. She rocked slightly as her fingers danced across the keys like she was playing the keyboard.

Reese climbed out of bed and pulled on her clothes from the night before. The wooden floor was cold beneath her feet. She scrubbed her hands over her face and ran her fingers through her mass of curls, but it was hopeless. She snagged a hair tie that was sitting on Arden's nightstand and gathered her hair into something that was a close approximation of a bird's nest.

Arden was still typing. Reese walked toward the door where her shoes and coat were waiting for her. She'd say bye on her way out. Maybe Arden would want to make plans for later, but it would be ok if she didn't. She probably had work to do. And Reese would be fine spending the day alone. She could call Lo back.

Something moved in her peripheral vision and she yelped as warm arms wrapped around her waist, pulling her down. Arden adjusted the blanket so it was around both of them. Reese let herself relax into the warmth of the wool and Arden.

"I didn't know this desk chair turned."

"I didn't know you would try to sneak out."

"I was letting you work."

"No, I was letting you sleep." Arden placed a soft kiss on the back of Reese's neck.

Reese ran her hands down Arden's thighs beneath her. She was in underwear and a loose shirt. Lingerie was sexy, but there was something so intimate about seeing what someone wore when they were home alone.

"So what do you want to do today besides escape?"

"Don't you have to work?"

"Do you want me to have to work?"

"No, actually. I want you to show me your life. But I understand if you have to write today."

"I did write today." She nodded toward the computer as her hands drifted under the hem of Reese's shirt. Her thumbs caught the waistband of Reese's jeans pulling it away before letting it fall back. "Why so many clothes?"

"It's cold in here."

"It is," Arden said as she rested her chin on Reese's shoulder, "but that's not why."

Reese let the silence stretch between them, waiting for Arden to break it, but she didn't. She let herself relax more fully into Arden. "I didn't want to bother you."

"Well, I want to be bothered. I hope you'll stay and bother me all day."

Reese tilted her head back and let it fall onto Arden's shoulder. She smiled at the ceiling, blinking away a tear in her eye. "That I can do."

. . .

"You really just want to do errands with me?" Arden furrowed her brows as they stepped onto the street outside her apartment.

"Whatever you'd normally do today. If that's errands then that's what I want to do. Think of it like you're giving me a tour of your New York. The attractions I want to see are where you go every day."

Arden laughed. "Usually hosting people is stressful because they want to go to Times Square or Central Park or the Statue of Liberty."

"Well, I wouldn't mind seeing that last one but not badly enough to deal with the crowds."

Arden looked deep in thought for a moment, her eyes narrowed before they widened with a brightness behind them. She gave a quick nod, "got it."

They spent the morning walking around Arden's neighborhood with coffee, taking a break to sit on her favorite park bench and eat the bagels they'd picked up. The park was a small one—almost a converted alley that cut between two streets. It had a narrow winding gravel path, a few bushes with snow clinging to their branches and a single anemic tree. People paid them no mind but several dogs greeted them enthusiastically as they passed by, dragging reluctant humans behind them.

"Are you sick of being outside yet?" Arden asked as they walked down another street of brownstones with their arms linked.

"Not at all. I can't believe there aren't more people out. I always think of New York like the subway at rush hour."

"I think the gray sky and snow are keeping everyone inside." A light dusting had drifted down to cover the sidewalk and speckle Arden's wool hat.

"Are you tired of being outside? Are you cold?"

"Nope. I brought my portable heater."

"Oh, did you?"

"Yup." Arden snaked an arm under Reese's leather jacket and pulled her closer. She'd kept it open, a large blue and green plaid blanket scarf she'd borrowed from Arden protecting her from the wind. "Ok then, I have an idea."

The streets might have been empty but the Whole Foods Arden had led her to was a three-story labyrinth of chaos. Every time Reese moved, someone pushed past her. Standing still was also no good. Arden kept darting off to grab things for the make-up picnic she'd proposed at a secret location she was "42% sure" Reese wouldn't hate.

A cart crashed into the back of her heels hard enough to make her stumble forward. She was in the dairy section looking at cheese and the passages were so narrow, shoppers had to turn sideways to avoid each other. All around her, precariously stacked displays dashed her hopes of a quick exit. Reese made herself as small as possible and waited for Arden to return. She'd asked Arden to give a tour of her life. Reese couldn't freak out in this grocery store—not when the day had been good so far.

A hand pressed between her shoulder blades and she flinched and stepped aside, muttering an apology.

"Hey, it's me. Are you ok?" Arden's voice was calm and steady. Reese closed her eyes and took a deep breath.

She nodded. She didn't trust her voice not to give her away.

"I hate this store, too. It's always mayhem on the weekends. And the aisles are like those playground tunnels. You practically have to crabwalk through this place."

Reese chuckled and felt something untwist in her chest. Her breaths were coming a bit easier now.

"I think we've got enough." Arden shifted the basket to her other hand.

Reese looked down at the few items in the basket but didn't argue. She'd much rather be hungry than have another panic attack in front of Arden.

"Come on," Arden said as she took her hand and cleared a path through the aisles like she was a fullback blocking the path for Reese's run. "Let's get out of here."

FIFTEEN

Liberty State Park was huge and cold and deserted. Fields and walking trails stretched along the shore of the bay for as far as Reese could see. Arden led them to a spot near the boardwalk, looking out at Ellis Island and the Statue of Liberty. The water was choppy and mirrored the gray sky. It was the perfect view with the perfect amount of other people around—one.

Arden paused, looking at the bits of brown grass sticking up from beneath the thin layer of snow. "I guess I should have thought to bring a blanket."

"You did." Reese unwound the scarf from around her neck and shook it out. The size of these big scarves was getting a little extreme.

Arden set down the bag of food and settled next to Reese, who had angled her back to the wind. The shopping trip had definitely gotten cut short and their provisions were eclectic as a result: cheese but no crackers, hummus with nowhere to go, a single orange, and two chocolate chip cookies.

Reese laughed as she took in the spread. "This looks like a kindergartner packed her own lunch."

"You haven't lived until you've tried hummus on cookies."

They ate and watched the few boats in the bay until the sun sank in the sky. By the time they were packing up, even Reese was willing to admit she was cold, though she would have stayed for hours with the way Arden was leaning into her for warmth.

"Where should I put in as the destination for the driver?" Arden had the app open on her phone. "Would you want to come back to my place for a bit or do you need some alone time?"

"Actually, would you want to go back to my hotel with me for a bit? I need to do a few things."

"I'd love that." Arden shook out the scarf and wound it back around Reese's neck before zipping up her coat beneath it. "I know you're cold. I could feel you shivering."

The hotel felt sterile and foreign after being at Arden's place. Reese took their coats as Arden walked straight to the bed and flopped onto it. "I forgot how tired the cold makes me. I feel like I could fall asleep right now." She shivered and pulled the comforter over her like a burrito.

"If you can stay awake a bit longer, I have a better idea."

Arden opened one eye and squinted at Reese. "I'm listening."

Reese ran the bath while Arden stayed in bed. She felt a little guilty shaking her awake once it was ready, but only until Arden sank into the hot water and sighed with relief. Arden let her head fall back against the edge of the clawfoot tub, her dark hair falling over the side in a mess of tangles from a day outside in the wind. Reese combed her fingers through Arden's hair and watched her eyes grow heavy.

Arden mumbled something unintelligible.

"What?"

"You should get in."

"Ok, but mostly to hold you up because you look very close to falling asleep."

"Be nice to me. I got up early to write."

Reese dropped her clothes to the floor and kicked them toward the corner before settling in behind Arden. As she leaned back, Arden pressed against her and the pressure of her hips between Reese's thighs lit something in her. She ran her hand through Arden's hair and gently pulled her head back to rest on her shoulder.

"Ok, there. Now you can fall asleep and not risk drowning."

Arden turned her head and placed a kiss on Reese's collarbone. "It's pretty hard to sleep with you like this."

"I thought you were tired."

"Yeah, well, something is waking me up."

Arden shifted until she was straddling Reese. Only spilling about a gallon of water on the floor as she executed the maneuver.

"Should I grab a towel?"

"I don't think that's the wetness we need to focus on."

Beneath the water, Arden's hand swam low across Reese's stomach. She braced her free hand on the tub next to Reese's head and leaned back a bit.

Her touch was gentle as she slid her hand between Reese's thighs. Reese let her head fall back as she sighed. Arden ran her fingers lightly over her clit before sliding her hand further down and entering Reese. Reese was suddenly starving for Arden.

She brought their mouths together, taking Arden's bottom lip between hers and biting it gently. Reese steadied herself with a hand on Arden's hip as she ran her other hand upwards starting from where she kneeled in the tub and making a slow path up her thigh and stomach before cupping her breast. Reese leaned her head down and drew Arden's nipple into her mouth. She gasped when Arden added a second finger but her mouth only lost contact for the briefest of moments before she returned her focus.

Reese let her hand descend to stroke the insides of Arden's thighs before moving upward. She dipped into Arden's folds and smiled at the heat she felt there, the distinct wetness coating her hand, so different from the water around them.

Arden picked up her pace, bringing her thumb to draw gentle circles on Reese's clit as she continued to fuck her. She was making it very difficult for Reese to focus but she was stubborn.

Reese entered Arden with two fingers and bit back a grin when her rhythm faltered. So much had changed since that first night in New York when Arden had shown up at her door, surprising Reese in this very tub. That stormy energy had always swirled between them. Where they had once been water and wind colliding, these weeks, all their scrimmages, had made their attraction stronger—a hurricane picking up strength over the open ocean.

As she came, Reese thought of the way Arden looked in the hotel hallway that night—confident and sexy and demanding. She stopped shaking in time to watch Arden throw her head back and gasp before collapsing against her and sinking her teeth into Reese's shoulder. Reese slowed her movements but kept her hand in place as Arden rode out her orgasm.

Arden righted herself and claimed Reese's mouth, her

tongue teasing her bottom lip before she deepened the kiss. "That was incredible. You are incredible."

Her fingers tangled in Reese's hair, tipping her head back just slightly. When their kiss broke, they were both flushed with ragged breaths. Reese drew back her hand and brought it to rest on Arden's hip, pulling her closer, feeling the heat of her arousal on her legs. Reese didn't trust herself to say anything because the words buzzing in her throat were huge and too soon and should never be said under the influence of orgasms. So instead she tucked a strand of hair behind Arden's ear and kissed her gently.

"You were right." Arden brought her forehead to rest against Reese's. "The bath was a great way to warm up."

SIXTEEN

The light in the room was murky. It reminded Reese of the way the water looked after cleaning paint brushes—all the colors coming together to make something disappointing. Even though the light was dim, she wanted to close the curtains so Arden could rest. She shifted, trying to ease herself out from Arden's limbs pinning them to the bed, but it was no use.

Arden made a soft noise next to her ear and Reese wrapped an arm around her like she was trying to help hold on to her sleep. "Sorry." She shifted some of her weight off Reese and her lungs filled with air. "You're a lot more comfortable than the bed."

"Yeah, they definitely went with cute over practical."

"Worked out for me. I wouldn't have pegged you as a cuddler, though." Arden adjusted her head on Reese's shoulder, placing a light kiss on her neck.

"I'm usually not, but I'm trying more things these days." Reese liked the warmth of Arden beside her. She liked never once having to wonder if Arden was still there because there wasn't a moment she wasn't holding on to

Reese. Sometimes even hugs made her feel trapped. But this felt like pure comfort.

They orbited around each other as they started the day.

"Do you want the shower first?" Reese said around the toothbrush in her mouth.

Arden smiled up from her phone. "Actually, I'm going to head to my place and then catch a meeting. I was just checking the schedule on my phone and there's one I like at 10. I probably won't be into the studio until closer to midday."

"Oh, should I text David that we'll be starting late?" Reese could always use the morning to catch up on work emails and line up other jobs. And she still needed to check back in with Lo.

"No, you two should get started. I trust you."

"Oh." Did Arden trust her because they'd slept together? Or because she finally thought Reese was doing a good job with the book? And did it really matter if it meant she got a morning of feeling competent with no interruptions? "Ok then. I guess I'll see you later."

Arden gave her a quick kiss and Reese closed the door behind her. She'd expected business Arden to return now that the weekend of fun was over. But this was something else.

ON HER WALK to the studio, her phone buzzed and her heart did a stutter step until she saw Judith's name on the screen.

"Good morning! Where do you keep your cream of tartar?"

"Hi Judith, I don't keep that anywhere."

Reese tapped the screen a few times as she navigated to her recent messages and pulled up her sister's name.

"Lo, did you leave Judith unaccompanied in the apartment?"

"Nope, we're hanging out."

"You're hanging out with my strange neighbor at nine am?"

"Babe, have you ever considered that you're the strange neighbor?"

"Why are you hanging out with her?"

"She's teaching me how to make her famous icebox cookies. She brought me some yesterday, they're amazing. I'm going to make some now for your birthday this year."

Reese would never understand her sister—the way she swung back and forth from the depths of her struggles to a bubbly Betty Crocker befriending local Judiths.

"Whatever you do, don't put her in charge of the oven."

"I don't think you're understanding icebox cookies, but ok."

"You'll probably need to go to the store if you're going to bake—I really don't have anything."

"That's fine. Judes just told me you don't have a single thing we need."

Reese held back an eye roll. Her sister did always love a nickname.

"Ok, be safe. I'm headed to work but text me a picture of the apartment later so I know it's still standing."

"Only if you text me a picture of yourself."

"Why?"

"Same reason."

. . .

DAVID LEANED back in the chair in the sound booth, hands behind his head and eyes closed. Reese pulled down her headphones and the light snore filling the small space confirmed her suspicions.

She placed a hand on his shoulder as she leaned close. "Sleeping on the job?"

He jerked awake, his feet clattering off the desk with a thud. "Hey Reesy. I was just resting my eyes until the boss gets here." He scrubbed a hand over his face and reached blindly for his coffee.

Reese grabbed the mug before it spilled and handed it to him. The liquid, a light tan, wavered in the mug imbuing the air with a scent as sweet as the air at a Yankee Candle.

"Arden's not coming in until later, but she said we can record this morning without her."

"How did you pull that off? And when did you talk to Arden?" David's eyes lit up. She needed to stop being friends with clever people who pay attention. David quirked an eyebrow at her, and she wished she had something unpleasant but harmless to throw at him. A pie, maybe. "You slept with her again?"

"What do you mean *again*?"

"I mean besides Saturday. Did you spend last night with her?"

"How did—wait, did you talk to Lo?"

"No, but thanks for confirming my theory."

"I confirmed nothing."

"Right," David said sarcastically. "I'm just kidding. I talked to Lo. She called me at the break of dawn yesterday to see if Arden was good enough for you or if she should airlift you out of New York before you get hurt."

It was a betrayal, but it was something else too. Something that felt warm in Reese's chest, her sister caring for her. Worrying about her. "Well, she can relax. It's just casual. There's no way I'm going to get hurt."

"Just be careful, babe. You take it hard when people let you down."

"Doesn't everyone?"

"Sure, but it's more for you. Arden's great, but she's not perfect."

His comment about Arden hit like ice, freezing out the warm feeling from a moment before. No one was perfect. She certainly wasn't. And besides, she'd just told him there was nothing to worry about. It was a little fun with a clear endpoint like a day trip to Coney Island. "Can we please get to work?"

By LUNCHTIME, Arden still hadn't shown up and David had an appointment, so Reese grabbed a sandwich and put on her white noise playlist as she caught up on some work.

A ping drew her attention and a photo of Judith doing a ta-da! pose in her kitchen filled her screen. "Ok, everything's still standing, including us! Now send me a picture of you."

Reese felt ridiculous snapping a selfie in the studio, but at least no one was around.

"I thought you'd look happy."

"Happiness is a fairy tale sold to us by greeting card companies and tampon commercials."

Lo's three dots appeared on the screen before disappearing again. A second later, a call was coming through.

"Relax, Lo. That was a joke. I'm very happy, I just don't need photographic evidence of it. I don't want Judith to print it out and start shopping me around to every single queer woman she runs into."

"Funny you should mention that. You didn't tell me your Judith is Judith Gross!" Lo's tone was a glitter bomb of excitement. But why was she saying Judith's last name like it meant something?

"Yes, I did. I talk about Judith all the time."

Lo sighed in exasperation, a sound Reese knew all too well. "Yeah, you talk about your horrible, annoying, way-too-kind neighbor Judith but you never mentioned that she's THE Judith Gross."

"I have no idea what you're talking about. It's a fairly common last name, so I assume she's not the only one. But how do you even know her full name?"

"This is why you need to talk to people, Reesy. You've been living next to a legend. She's Judge Judes."

"Who?" Lo's tone suggested she was clarifying things for Reese, but she still felt like the entire middle part of the puzzle was missing.

"Judge Judes! Don't you remember that radio show we used to listen to late at night when we were kids? Where people would call in with their problems and disputes, and she'd—"

"Solve them with kindness. Oh my god, Lo, I live next to Judge Judes."

"That's literally what I've been saying for five minutes. Honestly, I think it says a lot about how impossible you are that she hasn't reformed you yet."

"You always thought she was so wise, but I always thought she was—"

"Full of shit, I know." Lo chuckled.

"But that still doesn't explain how you even ended up meeting her."

"Ok, don't be mad—You know how I asked to stay at your place for a bit while I figure things out?"

"I mean, you sort of just told me you were there but I'll allow it."

"I couldn't find my key, so I was trying to break in with my library card. I forgot you have a million locks. Judes saw me in the hall and gave me her key."

"It's not her—you know what? That doesn't matter. Her key privileges are completely revoked. You could have been anyone."

"Right. I could have *been anyone* who looks just like you and is one of probably two people who know where you live."

"I hate your logic, but it's hard to argue with. Look, Lo, I need to do a few things before I get back to work. Please behave."

"I will! Judes is coming over later to watch Thelma and Louise, but after that I'm going to talk her into watching The Craft."

"You're going to watch The Craft without me?"

"Something tells me you'll be a little tied up tonight with your new beau."

Reese tried to keep the jealousy smoking in her chest from clouding her voice. "You're right. I'm glad you're having a good time. I'll check on you tomorrow."

SHE FELT the warm press of a body on her back and looked up to see Arden's chin tucked on her shoulder. "Reese, can you take those off?" When did Arden get there?

Arden stood up and mimed taking off headphones.

Reese closed her eyes and let the silence stretch out for a few seconds longer before she slid off the headphones. The cool air of the room assaulted her ears. Arden started talking immediately, but she was still blissfully muffled like she was underwater, her noise held at bay. She was still reeling from her call with Lo. It was not realistic to feel like her sister was replacing her with a retired radio personality, but knowing that to be true and feeling it were two different things.

She held up a finger as she pulled the earplugs out of her ears one at a time.

Arden tilted her head to the side, her brows drawing together. "Wait. You were wearing headphones and earplugs?"

"Yup."

"How did you hear your music?"

"These just filter sound, they don't block it entirely." Reese held up the small clear earplugs for Arden to see. "But to answer your question, I wasn't listening to music."

"Oh, what were you listening to then? A podcast?"

"Nothing."

"Ok, you don't have to tell me. I was just curious." A look of hurt passed across her face that Reese felt squeeze her chest.

Reese felt a spark of guilt in her stomach even though she had answered the question. Usually she'd let it drop, not caring if someone understood or got to know her. Mostly, she wanted the exact opposite of that. But something was making her want to explain and there was no harm in opening her door to Arden just a little more. She could leave the security chain on. "I did tell you. I wasn't listening to anything."

"Oh, so white noise? Like rain or car engine sounds." Arden looked like she was trying to make sense of Ikea instructions.

"Car engine sounds?" Reese couldn't suppress a laugh. "I don't think those count as soothing to most people. But no, I was listening to nothing as in silence. I didn't have anything playing."

"Oh, that's... interesting."

"I find it... a lot to be around people so much. And I'm a little out of practice. And on top of that, I just had a weird call with my sister who is now best friends with my meddling neighbor Judith. So I turned on the noise cancellation for a few minutes of silence—I figured I could quickly recharge before I needed to get back to recording."

"In that case, I'm sorry I interrupted."

She actually looked sorry, concern dug little trenches between her brows. It felt oddly endearing to have Arden understand. Like the comfort of a hug but better because no one was touching her.

"Can I ask one more question?"

And Reese found rather than just tolerating Arden's questions, she was actually curious what it would be. She nodded in a way she hoped was encouraging.

"You do it not to be anti-social but so that you can be social for longer?"

"Exactly."

"So it's like stepping outside for air, only it's more stepping inside for quiet." Arden's words were without judgment like Reese's logic made sense to her. "Do you want to get back to work or do you need more time?"

"Nah, I'm good now that you're here."

SEVENTEEN

Reese pulled up the chapter Arden had asked her to read and quickly scanned her notes for the first few paragraphs. She hadn't anticipated getting to this scene today, but the morning had been productive and who was she to argue if Arden wanted to go out of order. She probably had a good reason. It was nice to see her being less rigid with the project, especially after a weekend of her being downright flexible.

Reese had the nagging feeling that something big happened in this chapter that she wasn't quite remembering. Reading scenes she wasn't prepared for was something she would have refused a week ago. She looked up at Arden, her hair was falling tousled around her shoulders like Reese's hands had only just left it had her mind a little hazy. If Arden had requested sex in the glass fishbowl of the booth, she might have agreed.

Reese took one last sip of her water and began.

By the time she was halfway through the chapter, she was moaning as Sarah was pushed up onto the kitchen counter, dinner forgotten on the stove. Reese realized very clearly what Arden had done. She wanted to be frustrated but the visceral response of her body wouldn't let her.

Each time she ventured a glance up, Arden was staring at her and looking very pleased with herself. The heat of a blush warmed her face. Arden in her big studio headphones trying to look serious while she looked like she was struggling to sit still was making the words in front of her vibrate with excitement. No, not the words, just her hands as she tried to hold the screen steady. It was deeply unfair for a person to be that fucking adorable and also sexy. People should have to choose.

Reese missed a sentence and fucked up another while watching Arden. She took a deep breath as she redirected her focus to the words in front of her. She'd need to do it all again, even the orgasm. She kept her eyes on the screen and got back to work. She had some convincing moans to conjure up.

When she looked up again, she was surprised to see David had returned from lunch. She must have been focused on Sarah's climax, which was honestly a little dialogue-heavy for her tastes. He was sitting next to Arden, cheeks glowing. Reese didn't blame him, her performance had very much been for Arden's benefit.

David's voice piped in over her headphones. "That was, uh, great Reese. Truly never thought I'd be saying that to you about a sex scene but well done with the sounds and everything. I'll never be able to unhear any of it. Let's take a fifteen-minute break."

"Thanks. Let's never discuss this again." Reese pulled off her headphones and her phone buzzed immediately. Arden's name appeared on the screen and her heart did a little skip.

"That's not what you sounded like in my bed."

"Was it more convincing or less?" Reese caught Arden's eye and winked. She shook her head at Reese and lowered her gaze to her phone.

"Very funny. Maybe I need a refresher."

"I think that can be arranged, we do have fifteen minutes."

"Excellent. I'd like to get Sarah out of my head and you back into it. Meet me in the bathroom."

Reese was trying to figure out a clever response when her phone buzzed again.

"Please."

This was new to Reese, excitement accompanying a phone vibrating rather than dread. That little jolt near her hip edged toward erotic when she read Arden's message. The woman who had fucked her senseless the night before was now very kindly asking for bathroom sex. Reese was surprised to find herself just as turned on by that simple *please* as she was by Arden's calm command last night and early this morning.

Reese did her best to walk to the restroom like a calm professional but inside her anticipation was cartwheeling down the long hall. She probably could have without drawing attention, the offices she passed were completely deserted, many were studios that got rented on a project basis. She'd read sex scenes hundreds of times, and this wasn't the first time she'd felt ready to go after reading one. But Arden watching her and knowing Arden wrote the words that had done this to her—wrote the build-up and satisfaction—was something else. As she read the chapter, she'd felt Arden's eyes everywhere like Arden was reading her.

She entered the restroom with a vision in her head of Arden perched on that beautiful marble sink while the cold tile of the floor dug into her knees. Arden was leaning against the wall with one knee bent, hands shoved into the pockets of her black skinny jeans.

Reese stared at Arden. She wanted to move toward her but her legs were not listening. Instead, she watched as Arden pushed off the wall and sauntered toward her. Arden traced her fingertips across Reese's bottom lip and down to her neck, finally stopping with her hand splayed across her collarbone. "You," Arden brought her lips to Reese's, "Are extremely talented."

Reese was pulled forward like a magnet snapping into place. She felt built to kiss Arden on an elemental level. Her mind cleared of its chaotic thoughts as she backed Arden up to the way-too-fancy-for-a-restroom couch. Arden stumbled slightly when her knees hit the cushion and Reese nudged her back to sit. Being taken by Arden last night had been fun, but now she was ready to take.

Reese slid on top of Arden, straddling her. She did her best to brace her weight on her knees, though the break in the cushions were requiring a lot of core strength. *Did she need to work out more?* Reese braced her palms on the wall on either side of Arden's head and dipped down to capture her lips which were already flushed and full from their hello kiss.

Arden's hands wrapped around her hips and with a sharp tug Reese tumbled into her. She buried her face against Arden's neck trying to suppress her laughter.

"Do you think you can be quieter than you were in the recording booth just now?"

"Hard to make that promise without all of the information. Besides, I was hoping to be the one making it impossible for you to keep quiet."

"I suppose that can be arranged. So long as I get another

turn later—maybe back at your hotel? Not to U-Haul you. There should really be another term for when you're away from home. Like a checked bag. We'll go with that—I don't mean to checked-bag you. So feel free to take back the invitation I so generously extended to myself."

"No, I'd love to have you at my hotel later."

Arden crashed her mouth into Reese's before easing up a bit. She ran her tongue along Reese's bottom lip and wrapped her hands in her hair. Reese leaned more deeply into the kiss, letting Arden support her weight as she rocked her hips forward. Her desire was like hot lava moving through her. There was no stopping it—the only path to survival was to clear the way.

Reese reached down to brace one hand on Arden's hip and ran her fingertips over the braided leather of the belt circling her hips. Reese hadn't worn a belt in years but at that moment she couldn't imagine anything sexier than easing open the buckle and removing it slowly, loop by loop. Or perhaps opening it and holding either end to pull Arden closer with each kiss. Many good options. Everyone should wear belts all the time. She had been missing out on so much all alone in her apartment.

Reese got to work. She had the buckle open in seconds with a flick of her wrist. She hadn't even broken their kiss to focus on the task at hand. Her pride swelled like a teenager in her halcyon days unhooking her first bra mid-make out.

She secured her grip before pulling Arden gently toward her as she rocked her hips forward. Even though Reese controlled the movement and knew that connection was coming, the spark it sent through her caused her to moan against Arden's mouth. Reese broke their kiss and rested her forehead against Arden's to catch her breath. The sound of a dramatic throat clearing behind her froze her inhale in her chest.

"Well, this isn't what I had in mind when David said you were taking a break."

Arden's face paled, wiped clean of all expression as she leaned to one side to peer around her at Sophia. Reese had known the woman for one day and already had no trouble identifying the cut of the smoky voice behind her. She didn't need to look but something in her felt defiant. She'd already noticed in her short time the way Arden's agent treated her—like a child who had just been caught stealing sweets before dinner. Not bad but naughty. In need of reform.

"Hi, Sophia."

Reese turned slowly and took in Sophia, her dyed blonde hair and a lavender skirt suit were an odd choice for late winter. Her matching patent leather heels had the sheen of a plastic Easter Egg. The way she carried herself was both superior and ridiculous.

"I hope it's ok that I interrupted your... whatever this is. I'm sure you wouldn't want to miss our meeting about the status of the project." She spoke only to Arden as though Reese wasn't even there. Sophia turned on her kitten heel and stepped back into the hall, holding the door ajar and glancing at the rhinestone watch on her wrist.

"Of course not." The light that had been dancing in Arden's eyes a few minutes before had been snuffed out. Not even a glowing ember remained.

Reese felt Arden shifting beneath her. Her mind knew the moment was over but her body had yet to get the message. When Arden rose a bit from her seat to fish her phone from her pocket, lifting Reese a bit as their hips came together she had to hold back another moan as the heat gathered low in her stomach.

Arden glanced at her phone and her face went pale as she thumbed through the messages. "Twenty-two messages? Really, Sophia? I've only been gone five minutes."

"David said it's been more like twenty. Let's go, Arden, it's business. You know that thing you've built your entire life around?"

"Ok, I'm sorry." The way Arden dropped her head damn near broke Reese's heart, but she took her cue as Arden shifted once again beneath her.

Reese moved off her lap as gracefully as she could manage. This is what she imagined being caught by your parents felt like, not that she knew from experience. A little shame. A lot of adrenaline rushing through her veins. And beneath it all a deep well of frustration.

Arden followed Sophia into the hall and the door shut behind her with a soft click. Reese flopped back onto the couch and pulled her phone out, wanting to send Arden something reassuring. Something to undo a little of Sophia's influence. An emoji seemed too silly. But words were escaping her. At last, she settled on "Later?" Hopefully, Arden had a second to glance at her phone before the pastel inquisition started.

By the end of the day, Arden hadn't returned and her text had gone unread. She headed out into the fading sun in the direction of her hotel.

EIGHTEEN

The red blinking light flashed for the third time as Reese tried to get into her hotel room. Couldn't the universe see that she was overwhelmed and just needed a fucking minute to herself outside of the chaos of this city and this day? The very last thing she wanted was to have any sort of interaction with the guy at the desk. She shook the card as though whatever magic it used to grant her entry was misaligned.

Her phone buzzed and her heart did a little somersault. She'd been doing her absolute best not to think about Arden since leaving work, not to hope she'd hear from her. She'd planned out a night of white noise and reading—the kind of night that had always been perfect to her. The second she saw Arden's name on the screen the somersault transitioned into a back handspring—an entire floor routine. She'd miss this chaotic feeling in her chest when this project and her time with Arden ended. It had managed to magically fix the door lock, anyway.

"Want to come over? I'm cooking dinner."

"Sure, I'll see you in a bit."

Reese resisted tacking on the 1,000 exclamation points that were hovering at the edge of her fingertips wanting to shoot off like fireworks.

Reese went into the bathroom and brushed her teeth. When she was done she slid it into the travel case and threw it into her bag along with a few other essentials. Was that presumptuous? Arden had only mentioned dinner. She dumped the contents of her bag out onto the white hotel bedspread and grabbed her wallet and lip balm, tucking them into her jacket pocket along with her phone. She wrapped Arden's scarf around her neck and was on her way.

Arden's apartment smelled great, like lavender with vanilla layered somewhere behind it. The apartment was pristine except for the kitchen where the counter was littered with a cutting board, knife and a few dishes.

Reese held out the bottle of sparkling cider she's picked up at the bodega down the block.

She leaned in and pressed her lips to Reese's, "Thanks for coming, where's your stuff?"

"Did I miss a text? Was there something else I was supposed to pick up?"

"No, like your clothes for tomorrow. I've got plans for us tonight."

Reese laughed against Arden's neck as she placed a kiss there. "I almost packed my toothbrush. But then I wasn't sure how you were feeling about things after your meeting with Sophia. And I didn't want to be presumptuous."

"I see. Good thing I got you a toothbrush then."

"You did?"

Arden let go of Reese and walked to the kitchen counter, she reached into a cloth bag and pulled out a blue toothbrush still in its packaging, extending it toward Reese like a flower.

A lump formed in Reese's throat. She would not get emotional over a toothbrush, even if it did somehow scrub away all of the doubts that had been littering her mind since this afternoon.

"Thank you." Reese cleared her throat. "Blue's a good color."

Arden looked like she might laugh but instead she shot Reese a kind smile then rounded the counter into the main part of the kitchen. "You're welcome. And now I'm going to immediately cash in on that goodwill I built up because I have lured you here under false pretenses."

"You just mentioned dinner." Reese raised an eyebrow, scanning the pots on the counter. Arden had definitely been cooking *something*.

Arden grabbed a pot by the handle and held it upside-down. The yellow contents didn't shift—never a good sign.

"Is that... mac and cheese? What's the green stuff?"

"I tried to make it fancier by adding broccoli, but something went wrong."

Reese laughed. "Yeah, babe, something definitely went wrong. Do you want to try to save it or do something else for dinner?"

"Do you really think you can save this?" Arden pulled the spoon out of the pot with a sound like a boot in the mud.

Reese gave the most reassuring nod she could manage and walked to the fridge to examine the contents. "Definitely. Why don't you open the cider and tell me about your meeting with Sophia."

"Not much to tell, we just checked in on the project and

completion date. We've got the launch party coming up, so it's important for everything to be done by then. It's a big opportunity to prove myself again." Arden's delivery was wooden, like she was reciting lines without considering the content. She didn't pause at all.

Reese continued stirring and adding ingredients as Arden talked. She tried to puzzle out what to make of her shifted affect. Hopefully the conversation could be saved too.

Reese handed her a bowl of resurrected mac and cheese and took the open seat at the counter. Greek yogurt really was a miracle food.

"Well, we're in pretty good shape and we've made up a lot of ground in the last few days despite our setbacks and you requesting an out of sequence sex scene reading today."

"That was fun wasn't it?" Arden took a bit of dinner and her eyes lit up. "Are you a witch? How did you make this edible?"

"Dairy and Tajín, which I was very surprised you had."

"Why? Tajín is good on everything: fruit, rice, popcorn, this pasta situation."

"The Pasta Situation sounds like the name of an 80s band."

"You're right." Arden pulled out her phone and typed something into the notes. "Maybe I'll steal it for a book."

REESE REFILLED their glasses while Arden started washing the dishes. Reese took a seat on the emerald green velvet couch and sent off a quick text to Lo to see how her day had been.

The bubbles had started to fade from her cider like hot tub jets turning off, but Arden still hadn't joined her. Reese made her way over to the kitchen. Arden was staring out the window. The city sky at night was a particular kind of darkness—not complete, just dim, like a phone screen with the brightness turned way down. Small flakes of snow fell like static.

"Earth to Arden."

She turned and smiled at Reese over her shoulder as she reached to turn the water off. "Funny, I was just looking at the moon."

"What were you thinking about?"

"I've been kind of stuck on a scene I've been trying to work through. Actually, would you maybe help me with it?"

"Sure. Although I'm not sure how much help I'll be."

Arden took a few steps forward and wrapped the towel she had been using to dry her hands around Reese to pull her forward. "Oh, I think you'll be quite helpful."

Reese furrowed her brow and then laughed. "Wait, is it a sex scene?"

"Of course, it is, but we don't have to... if you don't want to." A blush burned on Arden's cheeks. "I just need help moving through it."

"I mean it would be a shame to put in all that effort and then not... you know."

The green leaves of the hanging plant were glossy beneath Reese' fingertips as she brushed them away from the window to look out at the street below. Her mouth had gone dry as Arden led them to her floor-to-ceiling window. And now that Reese was here watching herself reflected in the glass, and taking in the people on the street below she felt nervous. She grasped for something to calm her racing heart. "I always seem to kill my plants, what's your secret?"

"Sunshine and a lot less attention than you think they need. Plants are a lot like people that way."

It wouldn't be long until Reese was back in her apartment surrounded by her overwatered plants; both of them needing both more and less attention simultaneously. At least they could recover together. Leaving New York gave her a hollowed out feeling in her chest that she imagined transplanting a cactus into. At least the environment would be arid and inhospitable.

But if this was built to last it wouldn't be fun. Fun is only fun because it's fleeting. That's what makes it special. So she decided to let it be special because they had a scene to workshop. She focused back on the street outside, little bits of white dancing in the streetlights. "The snow is a lot more beautiful when it's not stinging my face."

"Yeah."

"From up here the snow makes everything look clean. I don't always love the cold but I do love the fresh start snow gives everything it touches. It's a gift."

"I guess we could all use a fresh start sometimes." Arden said. "Just the freedom to be whoever we want even if it's only until the snow melts."

Reese thought she caught a far-off look in her eyes, but maybe the reflection was bouncing off the glass like a funhouse mirror.

Reese turned and took a half step toward Arden. Arden grabbed her hips roughly, her eyes nearly black in the low light of the apartment.

Something had sparked beneath the surface of her calm exterior and Reese felt a sudden and desperate impulse to draw it out of her. To make her scream it into the room.

She brought her mouth to Arden's, crashing their lips together. Reese turned them around like a slow dance, hands on hips, thighs sliding into position as she backed Arden up against the window. She very much wanted to watch the snow fall behind her until the window clouded from the heat of their bodies. Reese saw it playing like a movie in her head, Arden's head resting on the cool glass as Reese fucked her. Is this what writing was like for Arden— just watching the scenes play out?

The heat of their bodies flared—and Reese felt a fierce warmth in her stomach like a match striking and igniting, the flame getting closer and closer to her skin.

She wanted to strip down and bathe in the glow of this heat. It was as though all of those days alone in her apartment were pleasant but muted—an impressionist painting of happiness. But now—she bit Arden's lower lip and watched it bloom poppy red—everything had the bright excitement of pop art, colors electric against the bright white canvas of the snow blanketing the streets below.

She thought back to her nerves about reading Arden's sex scenes in front of her and it seemed so trivial now. What was she doing? What would her sister say? For the first time in a long time Reese found she didn't care. She didn't want to be the one holding it together while everyone else got their reckless spinouts. She wasn't feeling any of the usual pressure she felt when outside of her apartment. Here in Arden's studio with the single streetlight outside lighting the snow-covered ground like a spotlight, she felt at home.

Arden moaned as Reese bit her neck pulling Reese back into the moment as she soothed the mark with her tongue. "Sorry," she said, kissing the dotted line again, signing it with her kiss. "Do you want it slower? Softer?"

Arden grabbed Reese's wrists and reversed their positions. Reese felt the cool glass through her sweater like a breeze.

"Hey Reese?" Arden said as she wove her fingers into Reese's unruly curls and tested her grip.

"Mm, yeah." Reese choked out her response, pain blending into desire.

"I'm going to direct this time."

Arden's hands were cool as they slipped beneath Reese's sweater. The goosebumps rippled across her skin as fingers raked up her stomach to cup her breasts, the slight sting of pain turning to fire in her veins. This was not how she had imagined this playing out. It was better.

Arden pressed a leg between Reese's until her knee made contact with the glass, pinned her more firmly against the window. She widened her stance to regain her balance and Arden immediately moved closer. The metal grid separating the panes of glass etched itself into Reese's back. She relished that little bit of discomfort grounding her in the present.

Arden braced a hand on the glass and shifted her leg upward. Reese's moan echoed. In that moment she wanted nothing more than to be taken. To be made to stand through it. To be held up as she came apart at Arden's touch.

This situation—Arden—was the destruction of her carefully ordered life; not in a slow unraveling, not in a carefully planned test trip to the grocery store, but in a complete explosion that had her feeling high and free and reckless.

Reese snaked an arm up her own sweater and covered Arden's hand with hers. Through breaths labored with want she managed, "This is crazy, right? But the good kind?"

"The best kind, now turn around." Arden's voice was firm and commanding and a little deeper than before. A near growl. Arden removed her hands from Reese's breasts and she felt their absence immediately. Reese let out a soft hiss when her nipples, still hard and almost aching, brushed against the stiff black lace of her bra.

Reese faced the window—she wasn't always bad at receiving orders. She almost didn't recognize the woman in the glass—her full lips parted with want, hair wild, back arched.

Arden's hands slid along her arms until she caught Reese's wrists and pressed them against the cold glass of the window. She leaned back and examined her work before repositioning Reese's hand slightly so both were centered in the fourth windowpane from the top and second from the edge, perfectly framed by the Rubrik's cube of black metal brackets.

Reese gazed at her own hands and felt a flood of arousal hit low in her stomach then radiate downward. "I'm down for precision even if I feel a little bit like you're setting this up to write it into a book later."

"Is it a problem if I am?" Arden said and Reese felt the nip of teeth on her shoulder.

"Not a problem at all, but how will you thank me in the acknowledgements?"

"I think we're still figuring that out." Arden trailed a hand down Reese's stomach as she spoke. Reese shuddered against the touch. She moaned as Arden pressed her hips hard into her ass and wrapped a steadying hand around her hip. Arden's fingers dug into the fabric of her jeans for purchase she felt both protected and so turned on she might melt.

Her free hand wove into Reese's hair and she inhaled sharply as Arden pulled her head back harder than she expected. Just a quick burst of pain that evolved into desire, coursing through Reese.

"Too much?" Arden whispered, sending warm breath washing over her neck.

"No, I like it, but—" Reese's words were cut off by a

moan as Arden licked a slow path from her ear to her shoulder.

"But?"

"Maybe a safe word," Reese gasped.

"Should we stop?"

"Please don't stop. Don't even slow down. The word can be window. I don't fucking care. Probably won't need it. It's just—I've read your books, I know how far this can go." Reese gasped again as Arden leaned over her and she felt the press of her breasts on her back. She wanted her shirt off so desperately she wondered if her thoughts were powerful enough to shred it like the Hulk. "Just in case you get carried away. Or I do."

"Here's hoping one of us does."

Arden sank to her knees and slowly slid Reese's pants down her legs, letting them pool around her ankles. "Let's take these all the way off, shall we? I wouldn't want you to fall."

For a moment Reese considered resisting. There was something erotic about the idea of being confined, limited in her movements as Arden took her. But the thought of losing her balance won out.

She worked her legs free of the pants. Arden paused to gently place a kiss on the back of each of Reese's knees before nipping at the inside of her thigh. She continued kissing upward until she got to the waistband of Reese's underwear and caught the black lace with her teeth and tugged it down in a quick movement, like tearing open a package.

Arden ran her hands up the insides of Reese's thighs until her fingers made the slightest contact with her center. Reese shuddered despite herself. In the glass she watched

Arden lean to one side and bite her hip before urging her legs a bit wider.

"Good girl," Arden said, placing a kiss on the small of Reese's back as she rose to her feet.

She slid her hands under Reese's sweater and pulled it up. The heat of Arden's mouth against her shoulders made Reese shiver. She reached around to cup Reese's breasts before pushing the bra up but not off. Arden studied their reflection. Running her fingertips along the black straps on Reese's bra, that ran parallel to the window. "I like this symmetry," she said in a whisper against Reese's neck.

Reese needed Arden to touch her but she seemed focused on setting the scene, delaying the action until the sense of place was fully established.

The warmth of Arden against her back was like a blanket against the chill from the air beyond the window.

Reese turned to look at her again and quirked an eyebrow. "I think you're a little overdressed—care to join me in this complete exposure to your beautiful city?"

She grabbed Reese's chin, turning her head a bit more, and pulled her into a deep kiss. It was over too soon. She placed her index finger gently on Reese's jaw and turned her eyes back to face their reflections.

She unbuttoned her own shirt and let it fall from her shoulders as Reese watched. Arden reached behind herself not breaking eye contact and made quick work of her bra before tossing it aside. She reached out and ran her fingers over Arden's reflection. Stopping when she got to the button of her jeans and giving the glass an insistent tap.

"These stay on for now." Arden said with a grin. "Ok, keep your eyes forward, Ms. Walker. Is it weird to call you that?"

"Not at all Ms. Abbott."

Arden caught Reese's gaze in the window's reflection and Reese's breath caught. The night sky was a dark theater to watch the emotions play out between them.

She trailed a hand down along Reese's spine, over the curve of her ass and lower, nudging Reese's legs a bit wider as her hand slid between them and dipped into the arousal found there. The moan that echoed off the glass this time was not Reese's.

Arden pulled back slightly and refocused on their reflection before entering Reese hard and fast. Reese's gasp fogged the glass obscuring precious seconds of her view. As it cleared she looked into the fierceness of Arden's gaze studying her face.

Arden settled into a rhythm as the steam cleared. Reese pushed back into her and Arden brought her free hand up to grip her shoulder and direct her forward a bit more. The glass was growing warm where Reese's palms pressed into it, holding her up as Arden continued to move with her.

Reese took in the sight of herself, bent over in front of Arden, hands slipping slightly down the window and her messy red curls as wild as Medusa. A sharp spark of want hit her core like lightning just before the sky opens up.

Arden curled her fingers and trailed her hand down until her fingers found Reese's clit. Reese cried out and jerked into a new rhythm. Arden pressed her a little closer to the glass and moved her hand away from her clit to her hip to steady her. Reese's forearms now rested on the cool slick surface as she met Arden's eyes.

"I'm not sure I can stand much longer with you—" her words were cut off as Arden added another finger. The heat of her skin warmed Reese's back as she leaned forward and bit Reese's neck just below her ear. Arden maintained her focus on that spot as she slid her fingers from Reese' hip to between her thighs again.

"I better hurry up then," Arden whispered against Reese's ear as she began to circle her clit softly at first. Reese could feel Arden's eyes on her, studying each shift in her reflection like she was taking notes.

Arden focused her movements and timed them with each thrust. She increased her speed. Reese's legs were struggling to hold her up, but she knew she would trust Arden not to let her fall.

"Look at me." Arden was smiling as Reese opened her eyes. "I want us both to remember."

She added a third finger as she continued to circle Reese's center. Reese threw her head back and cried out. The echo of her scream off the glass filled the apartment like a symphony of pleasure. Arden stilled her hand but remained inside as Reese tightened around her and let out shuddering breaths as she came back to herself. She reached up to gently brush Reese's hair from her face before she brought their lips together tentatively at first and then hard enough to swallow any other sounds.

When Reese stopped shaking, Arden broke their kiss even though she was hungry for more. "Are you steady enough to stand on your own?"

"I suppose I can if I have to, though that was a valiant effort to make standing impossible," Reese said with a smirk. "Why, what's next?"

"Next, I take you to bed."

NINETEEN

Reese woke up to an empty bed, dim morning light streaming through the windows. This was getting to be a normal thing, waking up alone in Arden's bed, and she found she didn't mind it. She stretched out, the cool sheets caressing her naked skin. She liked starting the day with a few moments to herself, and a quick replay of the night; memories trailing like fingertips across her body as she allowed herself to once again feel Arden everywhere. She examined a mark on her collarbone, a palimpsest of Arden burying her face there as she came beneath Reese.

A groan from the desk drew her attention.

"Everything ok over there?"

No response except Arden's typing steady as the beat of rain on a car roof interrupted only by the gusts of her sighs.

Reese threw on a t-shirt and underwear and made her way to the kitchen in search of coffee. At least she didn't have to worry about disturbing Arden. She was in her own world, sealed in by her headphones and her focus.

When the French press was ready, she grabbed two mugs and carried one over to the corner of the desk.

Arden slipped her headphones off, and Reese heard the crackle she'd been listening to. "White noise?" Reese tilted her head to the side. Since when did Arden listen to anything other than instrumental music when writing.

"Yeah, I've been trying it out. I'm spinning in circles in this scene and music wasn't helping. It's that silence playlist you shared with me."

"Ah, Must Love Silence, all the greatest hits of pure nothingness. So many bangers on there."

"I like Great Lake, Cold Night the best." Arden wrapped an arm around Reese's waist and pulled her close. Her hand strayed down to the bare skin of Reese's thigh. "Aren't you freezing in this?"

"Nope." Reese placed a kiss on the top of Arden's head. "So what's going on with this scene?"

"You're really going to help me with another scene? After last time?"

"I'd help you with a hundred scenes, a thousand, after last time."

Arden sat up a bit taller in her chair, a smile pulling at the corner of her lips. She jotted something down in the notebook beside her before flipping it over. "Noted."

"So what's going on?"

"It just feels off, like the tone isn't fitting."

"Do you want me to read it to you so you can hear where it's working?"

"You'd do that?"

"Of course. I love to read."

Arden's fingertips were cool as they ran over the skin of Reese's hip.

"You have to behave though, so I can concentrate."

"Deal." Arden pulled Reese onto her lap and reached around her to scroll up to the beginning of the chapter.

"What's this one called?"

"Love Bites, it's about a perpetually single radio host who gives love advice to random callers, some of it good, some of it bitter."

"I love it. Ok," Reese said as she took a deep breath and increased the font size a few points. "Here we go."

"HI, caller, you're on the air."

"Hi, my name is Joan. I just started seeing someone new and I find myself getting lost in her. I'm wondering how to balance that early bliss stage in a relationship where it's hard to hold on to your identity because all you want is to be near this other person."

"Well, if we believe the fairy tales or the nightmares, sometimes those feelings never go away. But the way I see it is relationships are work, but it should be like saving seats."

"What does that mean?"

"Think about going to the movies with your partner. Maybe they're getting popcorn and hopefully Junior Mints. The point is, when you walk into the theater, you scan for two seats together. You make sure you each get a seat. You're always thinking about your partner, considering them and their needs, but alongside your own. We need both seats to enjoy the movie. But what you're doing is standing in the aisle, holding her coat. She probably wants to enjoy the movie with you. In this metaphor the movie is your relationship, it's life, and love. You've got to make sure you have a seat too, Joan."

.   .   .

REESE REACHED where the page ended, an unfinished line, and a blinking cursor. "I thought it was good. I like how the host is kind of gruff on the surface—even her metaphor doesn't sound sweet on the surface, but it is when you go deeper. It's about loving yourself too."

"Yeah."

"You still sound unsure."

"Isn't romance supposed to be this big, all-in, no doubts thing? Maybe I'm too jaded to keep writing love stories."

"Not at all. The struggle is what makes the payoff so sweet. And I like Joan, I like that she's grappling with that feeling people usually relish getting lost in. I like that she sees herself as worth holding onto."

"Yeah." Arden brought her chin to rest on Reese's shoulder and wrapped her arms more tightly around her. "Me, too."

THE DAYS WENT by like quicksand, mornings to afternoons to evenings slipped through her fingers as she tried to grab their time together and hold onto it.

It was the day before Arden's book launch party when they wrapped up the recording, sliding in just under the wire. Narrowly avoiding being garroted by Sophia. Arden had missed the last day, some sort of planning meeting with Sophia she'd been very vague about in the shower that morning.

Reese knocked on the door to the sound booth and waited for David to nod before easing open the door. "Want to grab lunch?"

"I wish I could but I really want to get these chapters

edited so I have something to turn over to Sophia tomorrow. But I'll see you at the launch party, right?"

She studied the scuffs on her boots, the idea of getting a shoeshine that afternoon floated through her head like she was some 19th-century businessman.

"You still with me, Reese?"

"Yeah, I'm not sure about the launch party. I haven't exactly been invited."

"Don't be ridiculous. Arden would want you there. She probably just assumed you'd be going with her."

"What if she didn't? I'm not sure we're in the same place. I've been thinking about asking her to try long distance. She'll be in Chicago soon for her book tour anyway. But sometimes I can't read her. I either feel like she never wants me to leave or is just waiting for our time to run out so she can get back to her life."

"I have an idea."

"What's that?"

"Talk to her. And don't miss her launch party."

"I don't have anything to wear."

"Good thing we're done early and you have the whole afternoon to go shopping in one of the fashion capitals of the world."

She knew David was right. Just like she knew Lo was right. Just like even Judith might possibly be a little right. Maybe people weren't all terrible. Maybe she deserved a shot at happiness, but she'd never get it if she didn't ask. But first, she had an outfit to buy.

TWENTY

"I don't understand why a party for *you* is at a bar."

Arden's book launch was that night and Reese had thought of little else since the night before. Each hour closer the party, some new concern revealed itself to her like a terrible nesting doll of anxiety.

The conversation she'd had with Lo the night before when Arden was in the shower did not make her feel better. When Reese had mentioned that Arden's book launch event was at a bar Lo's long silence had magnified every speck of doubt that had been quietly floating in her mind since she'd found out.

"Where else would it be?" Arden threw herself back against the pillows on her bed, eyes focused on the ceiling. One sentence into the conversation and she already seemed exasperated.

"Literally anywhere else. A bookstore, maybe? You know, a place dedicated to selling books." The rug was warm beneath her feet as she paced in front of the couch, doing her best to look serious in only her underwear and a thin t-shirt. A power outfit, but not in this situation.

"You're being really intense about this, Reese. It's going to be fine. I'm going to be fine. Relax."

Reese unclenched her jaw. "I am relaxed." How could Arden not see she had a point? That she was just worried about her being at a bar for a big moment when nerves would be running amok. This wasn't control, this was care.

"I can see you gritting your teeth from all the way over here. Why are you so far away?" Arden patted the bed next to her.

Reese kept walking. "So, you're telling me you're not nervous *at all* about having to spend a stressful night at a bar surrounded by people who are drinking? Will you leave if you get overwhelmed?"

"I'm really not nervous. And of course, I won't leave. I'm a professional. Sophia put a ton of work into this event for me. I have something to prove tonight. To her but also to myself." Arden sat up in bed, the sheet falling to her waist, her hair in a ponytail that had slowly migrated to the side as she slept. She was perfectly disheveled, and it was goddamn distracting.

"Can we make a plan for what you'll do if you feel over-whelmed?"

"Reese, I know you mean well, but I don't need you to take care of me. I've gathered that's a role you're used to playing but I have an entire chat group of people to do that."

"You have a sober chat group?"

"Yeah, Champagne Problems. They're my friends from rehab. We strategize how to stay sober in difficult situations. But I'm feeling good, I promise."

"I'm having trouble getting over the fact that you named a sober chat group Champagne Problems."

"Well, we go by The Champs for short. Anyway, most people there don't even know I'm sober and I'd like that to still be the case at the end of the night. Please just go with me and support me. In the nicest way possible, I'm your girlfriend, not your sister."

"I know that. I mean I didn't know the girlfriend part, and we should talk about that. But I know your experience is different from Lo's. I'm just worried about tonight. I know I get intense when I care. You'll be back in the spotlight and I want to ease some of the pressure."

"Well, in that case, come here and ease it. I am nervous about the speech I have to give." Arden pulled the sheet aside revealing her bare legs. Her skin was luminous from the soft light streaming in through the large window. She opened her arms and Reese took a few steps toward her then faltered, her feet freezing in place.

"I just—"

"Reese Walker, stop worrying about tonight and get back into this bed. If you want to worry about something you can start by worrying about me right now."

As she dove into the bed and wrapped her arms around Arden, all she could think was that Arden had used the word girlfriend. Maybe asking to try long-distance would be less scary than she thought.

THE DAYS WERE SLOWLY GETTING WARMER, but winter still owned the nights. Reese's leather jacket was doing little to cut the wind as she made her way to Stonehenge bar.

Things had still felt unresolved when she'd left Arden's apartment earlier so they could both get ready. Well, some things were *very* resolved but her concerns about tonight and Arden's casual dismissal of them had been left suspended.

That she'd spent two afternoons in a row shopping for an outfit in actual stores had done little to improve her outlook. She's tried on pants in six different sizes because women's clothing used a tape measure straight out of Candy Land. The experience might have been a gauntlet but the hug of the black jeans on her body had her walking just a little bit taller. She'd paired them with a tailored white dress shirt and black boots. She felt put together just enough to help Arden shine.

The brass of the door's handle was cold beneath her palm as she hesitated to draw in a full breath of the night air. Arden had this covered. She didn't need anyone to take care of her. The world would not fall apart if Reese relaxed. Probably. She would try her best.

She checked her phone one last time but Lo still hadn't responded. She had sent her an eight-text-long draft of her "let's make a go of it" speech she planned to give Arden later.

Inside the bar was like a hipster Bennigan's, somewhere between actually old and artfully distressed. The music was loud and too upbeat for the event. Whatever happened to light jazz? The vibe was a bit more frat party than serious book event. The groups of people filling the space raised their voices to be heard over the music, shouting empty pleasantries to each other. Reese resisted the urge to turn around and walk back out into the freezing night.

She slid onto one of the few empty stools along the bar, quickly reaching for the wooden surface when her seat sunk a bit like a barber's chair. She surveyed the room, seeing overdressed groups of twos and threes clutching their drinks like lifelines, but no sign of Arden. At least there was a good turnout. The bass of the music crawled across her skin, and she had to force herself to be still. Tonight was for Arden—it didn't matter if it made Reese a little uncomfortable.

"What'll it be?"

The man had appeared out of nowhere like an apparition of a barkeep in some gold rush ghost town—his brown pants were held up by shamrock green suspenders. He smiled at her and his mustache dripped down his face like a melted candle.

"A seltzer would be great."

"Are you sure you don't want to take a look at the cocktail menu? There are a few free themed ones for tonight." He slid a small slip across the bar.

"Why would there be themed drinks for the book launch of a sober author?"

He shrugged causing one of his suspenders to slip off his shoulder, which Reese now realized were sloped and in no way could pull off his outfit. "I just serve drinks and do what I'm asked—that's kind of the whole gig."

"Got it." Reese pushed the card stock menu with a wedding invitation font back across the bar. "Just the seltzer, please."

The bartender swiped up the menu and turned to grab a glass, his small bun bobbing with his movements.

A weight settled onto her shoulder. "Are you going to wear this coat all night? I want to see what you're wearing." Arden's lips were so close that they brushed against Reese's ear. A shiver of anticipation ran through her. Arden on her back that morning as they put their argument to rest flashed through her mind. In three hours they could be through this and back in bed, making the most of their last days together before she went back to Chicago.

Arden's hands slipped under her leather jacket and over

her breasts before making their way to Reese's shoulders. Arden slipped off Reese's coat in one smooth motion.

"I went for simple," Reese shrugged as Arden's eyes roamed over her to take in her outfit.

"Classic. You look perfect." She leaned in and kissed just below Reese's ear hovering there to whisper, "Thanks for being here tonight. I know parties are basically torture for you."

"I wouldn't have missed it; I mean not unless you want to skip it altogether?"

"Not a chance. Do you have any idea how long it took me to get ready?" Arden twirled around. Her green dress was vibrant even in the dim bar light. It was a nice contrast to her dark hair, which cascaded around her shoulders in loose silky curls. Reese imagined running her fingers through them later and how chaotic they'd look tomorrow morning—fanned out over the pillow as the sun streamed in through the floor to ceiling window at Arden's apartment.

"You always look perfect, but I can see that you're wearing mascara."

Arden leaned forward and placed a chaste kiss on Reese's mouth before resting their foreheads together. "What am I going to do without these astute observations of yours when you go back to Chicago? Can't you just stay in New York?"

Reese turned on her stool so that Arden was standing between her legs.

"I was actually hoping we could talk about that. I wanted to wait until later but I—"

"There's my belle of the ball. You look fabulous darling. Did you see the drinks menu?"

Sophia's head came into view behind Arden's shoulder

like a clown playing peek-a-boo as she placed air kisses on both of Arden's cheeks. Horrifying.

"I didn't see the menu, but I'm going to stick with water tonight."

"At least get something in a fancy glass so it's not so obvious. You've got an image to uphold." Sophia wrapped an arm around Arden's waist and Reese felt her slipping away, the air of the bar suddenly cool against her legs.

Blood rushed in Reese's ears like ocean noise on her headphones. A sharp pinch of pain in her palms focused her. She unclenched her fist and took in the slivered moons of rage her nails had left behind. "Maybe it's time for Arden to build a new image? One that actually reflects who she is." She pulled a smile onto her face, but she knew it didn't reach her eyes, which she narrowed in the direction of Sophia's hideous skirt suit.

Arden shot Reese a warning look that could refreeze the ice caps. Had scientists considered employing pissed off girlfriends to combat climate change? At least the chill tempered her boiling rage, leaving her sitting in the steam of shame.

"I'm going to steal you away from your friend now, Arden," Sophia said as she held eye contact with Reese. "I want to hear your little speech. I'll have the bartender fix you something to drink and meet you in the back."

Sophia grabbed Arden's shoulders and spun her around. She placed a hand between her shoulder blades, nails blood red and talon-sharp. She gave Arden a firm push as she sent her as far away from them as physics would allow. She turned her back to Reese and leaned against the bar to flag the bartender's attention.

Reese tasted blood in her mouth and unclenched her jaw. She'd always thought biting your tongue was a metaphor, but in practice, it was a pretty painful tactic for self-restraint. Arden had asked for support tonight, not interference. She was completely, 100% capable of not interfering, even if Sophia was determined to be the worst.

The bartender leaned close as Sophia tapped something on the drinks menu that Reese wasn't able to see. That can't be right. All of the drinks on the menu had alcohol.

Drinks in hand, Sophia stalked after Arden. The red liquid in two martini glasses made Reese's stomach clench. She thought cosmos had stopped being a thing when Sex and the City went off air.

The need to do something—literally anything—to protect Arden from Sophia swelled inside her. She wanted to slosh that horrible cranberry liquid onto the floor. She gripped at the edge of the stool to hold herself in place.

Sophia slowly extending the glass to Arden was a car wreck in slow motion. And Reese was just watching it all happen from the side of the road when she could fix it in ten strides. The drink passed from Sophia to Arden, who squinted at it. Sophia laughed in response to something she said, and Arden shrugged as she raised the glass to her lips.

Reese was across the room before she'd even decided to get up. The cold liquid splashed across her palm as the glass crashed to the floor. Shards of glass shot everywhere shimmering to the ground like a firework falling from the sky, but the liquid sloshed mostly onto Arden's dress.

"What the hell, Reese?"

"Sorry, I didn't mean to spill it, I just..."

"You just what? What were you thinking?"

"I was thinking it looked like a drink."

"It was. It was my drink, that Sophia kindly brought to me. Fuck. What am I going to do about my dress?"

A wet spot bloomed above her heart, the fabric marred with the wound of a dark stain.

"I'll switch with you." Could that work? She and Arden were close to the same size, but besides sweats and t-shirts, the theory had never been tested. What better time than now? Maybe she could make up for her overreaction a bit.

"And you'll what? Wear a stained dress?"

"I guess," Reese tried not to shiver at the thought, at least she could throw her jacket over the worst of the stain.

The bathroom was empty, the music bouncing off the tan and green tile floor and walls to reverberate even louder than the bar. Reese turned the lock on the door so they could have a few Sophia-free minutes to sort this out. The drink had looked like alcohol.

What was she supposed to do, just let Arden drink it? "What if I just give you my jacket? I really don't want to wear that dress."

"Are you fucking kidding me right now, Reese?" Arden paused, one arm behind her awkwardly unzipping the dress. Goosebumps rose on her skin where the fabric had slid off her shoulders. "I think it's the least you could do. I told you I had tonight under control, but you couldn't let it go. I can't be with someone who doesn't trust me to take care of myself. That's not love, it's control."

"Ok, fine, I'll wear the dress." Reese's voice was muffled by the shirt stuck over her head. In her haste to course correct this conversation, she'd failed to unbutton it. Arden was talking about love like it was something slipping away from them instead of something they were just on the cusp of.

"No, Reese. It's not about the dress. Look, you don't want to be here. The book is done and you're heading back to Chicago the day after tomorrow. Let's just call it."

"Like call it a night?" Reese handed the shirt to Arden and shimmied out of her jeans.

Someone pounded on the door and a moment later Sophia's voice cut through all of the emotions swirling between them like a guillotine. "Arden, are you almost done in there? You really need to address everyone, then do the reading we selected. Or is your narrator doing that? Is that why you brought her?"

"No, she's not. I'll be right out Sophia. Two minutes." Arden's voice sounded like a wire about to break. She slipped on the shirt and jeans and ran her hands over her body to smooth out the wrinkles.

She turned her attention back to Reese and took the pants from her hand, hopping as she pulled them on.

"No, *call it*, call it. You can keep the dress. I need to go rehearse my speech and get another seltzer and cranberry juice."

"Arden, I'm sorry. I really thought it was alcohol and you were about to drink it because Sophia was pressuring you, or had lied to you or something."

"I know. That's the problem. I never needed you to save me. I needed you to meet me where I was and love me there." Arden's eyes looked haunted, emptied out of anything meaningful.

The words slashed Reese's chest, but she was silent. What was there to say when someone stabbed a dagger into a truth about you—that you didn't know yourself—and then dropped the terrible glistening mess of it at your feet?

Arden draped the dress over Reese's arm and walked out of the bathroom. The breeze from the swinging door raised goosebumps on her naked skin.

Reese leaned against one of the stalls, letting the cool metal sting her back. She watched the bathroom door for a few seconds hoping Arden would come back, but it didn't move.

This was always what happened, wasn't it? She let someone in, set down all the things that protected her, and then the knife twisted in.

None of this mattered. New York and Arden weren't real life. These past few weeks were a blip. A job that had gone too far and she'd somehow caught feelings. But she was the only one. Now she had to figure out a way to recover. Time alone and rest. Oh, and fluids.

She slipped on the dress, fighting every urge in her body to shred it like the Hulk. She was in the mood to destroy, to do anything to let off a little of this toxic sadness that was choking her. But mostly what she wanted was to leave.

Should she stay for the reading? Would it look weird if she left? Did she care?

The silk fabric of the dress slid over her shoulders and breasts like stepping into a cool stream. The adrenaline in her body had made her skin hot to the touch. The cranberry stain settled over her heart and she felt a bitter laugh she didn't recognize bubble up in her throat. The dress, the stain, all of it fit perfectly.

She walked out of the restroom and caught sight of Arden standing near the front of the room, water in hand, looking absolutely perfect in Reese's clothes. There was something so intimate about it—seeing someone you love in your clothes. The desire sent a new blade into her chest and her breath caught. The center of her chest felt like quicksand, an insatiable pit of emptiness pulling in the memories of the last few weeks and snuffing out their joy.

Reese knew she should feel bad that she intervened, but she didn't. It was who she was, fundamentally. And that's why the rejection was a switchblade that just kept contorting in her chest. Each inhale keeping the pain fresh. But maybe if she apologized again and found some miraculous way to prove that she could back off, then she could fix this. She took a step toward Arden. Then another.

Her phone buzzed in her hand and she glanced at the screen. She knew it wasn't Arden texting her; she'd just been watching her specifically *not* texting her. Still, in that second before her eyes made sense of the screen it felt like the blade piercing her heart had been drawn out a bit.

She saw the string of missed call notifications from Judith. How had she missed so many? She remembered setting Judith's calls not to ring after she called four times about a plant emergency during a recording session. The emergency had been that she couldn't remember if she had watered the plants that morning. Did Reese remember? She did not.

The text from Judith that lit up her phone read 911 and then (This is about Lo, not plants.)

A thousand terrible Lo 911s flashed through her mind in the time it took her to click on Judith's number and raise her phone to her ear. She pictured her sister lying drunk or hurt while she was at this party, selfishly worried about her own heart. But knowing Judith, it was probably nothing. Lo probably hadn't answered a text or had missed canasta.

"Reese, I'm so glad you called me back," Judith's voice was its usual breathless rush. She always found it grating but now her inability to parse her usual breathlessness from emergency breathlessness had her heart pounding in her ear.

"Is Lo ok?"

"I don't know." Reese could practically hear Judith wringing her hands.

"What do you mean you don't know?" Judith knew

everything. Down to the smallest minutia of Reese's daily routines.

"She's not answering the door."

That could mean anything. When would they invent the technology to be able to reach through the phone and shake someone? Reese paused. The relief that flooded through her weakened her knees and she leaned against a high top table. It was just Lo not responding to Judith. Reese did that a hundred times a week. A thousand. "O...k... She probably went out."

"No, I tried my key and the door is chained. But when I called her name she still didn't answer. I yelled as loud as I could. And you know that's loud."

Judith's opera singing came to mind and that, more than anything, sent Reese's heart to her throat. Unless you were in a coma there was no way to block out the voice of Judith. "How long ago was that?"

"Maybe an hour. I've tried a few times since then and even checked the balcony."

Ok, an hour was not that long. It was one Taylor Swift album, or one Taylor Swift song twelve times. "She seemed fine the last time I talked to her. A little tired maybe but solid otherwise." Was that yesterday? She'd been so caught up with Arden that she wasn't sure. "Do you think I should get someone to break down the door? Call 911?" Reese asked.

"No, dear. I just think someone should check on her. She seemed fine last night."

"You were with her last night?"

"Yeah, she's a whiz at canasta."

"Of course, she is."

"I know you're busy in New York, but I just didn't know what else to do. Maybe you can give her a call?"

Reese thought about what would happen if she called 911 and sent them barreling into her apartment. Would Lo be sitting there totally fine and feel violated by Reese like Arden did? She felt caught between two terrible options, one where she did too little and the worst happened. And one where she did too much and ruined another relationship.

Reese glanced at Arden. She watched her pull her hair up into a messy bun that managed to look sophisticated and sexy with the white shirt. The outfit she had so painstakingly picked out with the help of way too many sales associates to look just the right amount of professional butch somehow looked completely different on Arden. It looked softer, with a slight athletic edge. Like maybe she'd just come from visiting her horse. The pants clung to her and the first three buttons of the shirt were open.

Arden's words echoed through her mind. Maybe Lo didn't need saving. But what if she did?

"Thanks for calling me, Judith. It's probably nothing but I'm going to catch the next flight home. Everything I was doing in New York is over anyway."

TWENTY-ONE

R eese's eyes were bleary as she unlocked the deadbolt to her apartment. It was going on two am in Chicago and Lo's phone was still kicking straight to voicemail. With each useless ring, her stomach tightened, like a locked seatbelt constricting her movement more and more each time she breathed. The chain caught, jerking her momentum back into the hall. At least her sister was somewhere in the apartment. Was that better or worse?

When she left Chicago, both a few weeks and also a million years ago, Reese had expected finally getting back to her apartment would be like climbing into bed when the sheets are fresh. But this was not that. This was coming home from vacation to find a tornado had ripped her life apart.

Reese peered through the narrow gap between the door and the frame. A lamp in the corner gave her a murky view of the living room, its shade was askew and it threw weird shadows like light filtering through water. The white walls of that had always looked clean to Reese before now looked lifeless. She thought of the emerald green on the walls in Arden's apartment, glossy and lush like a rubber plant.

Lo had been staying at her place for less than a week, but Reese saw evidence of her everywhere through the cracked door. Pants draped over chairs, books scattered face down on the windowsill like birds that had flown into the glass. Her sister's presence layered on top of the still life of her perfect apartment like chaotic finger paint on a white wall.

A half-empty glass of water sat on the floor near the couch next to a pair of jeans that were resting directly on top of a pair of shoes. Ever since they were little Lo had shed clothes like she had been raptured, everything left in a pile as though she had shed her mortal coil on the spot.

Reese took a breath. Many signs of Lo were present: positive. Except for Lo herself: very much less positive. *What was she up to?* That was the $1,258 question that fueled her last-minute direct flight back from New York. She'd been stuck in first class, the only seat available, somehow both a hardship and a perk. She'd made two lists of explanations for Lo's disappearing act. One was called "normal explanations" and the other was called simply, "bad things that could happen". One list was significantly longer than the other.

First things first, she'd do a sweep of the apartment and hopefully not find her sister in some sort of distress or worse. As soon as she got the door open, that was. She closed her eyes, taking a break to steel herself. She felt the lack of Arden next to her like a black hole, an absence pulling her in. She pushed it away.

Reese slowly released the breath she was holding. The idea hit her and she felt ridiculous for how long it took. She pulled out her phone and found a man explaining in a lengthy video how to open a chained door from the outside.

She pulled the elastic from her hair and her curls bloomed around her face. Reese's leather jacket hit the floor with a thud as she threaded her bare arm through the gap. She wrapped the elastic around the end of the chain and the other end on the door handle before easing the door shut.

Reese held her ear close to the door and nothing. She pulled the door back toward her and the chain blocked her entry. She adjusted the hair tie so it was tighter, looping it around the doorknob a second time. She took a deep breath and held it as she eased the door shut. The clink of the chain that had kept Judith out dropped free and knocked against the frame of the old oak door, echoing in her head like a beating heart.

She let out her breath in a cough of relief and awe. This might have been the first time in history that a man on the internet gave her useful advice that she actually wanted.

Reese eased the door open an inch, then a foot, then a human-sized gap that she stepped though like a portal into the unknown.

She'd start in the living room and work her way through. She could check the bathroom last.

Reese left the door open, her bag and jacket abandoned in the hall. The light she flicked on burned her tired eyes. A figure shot up from the couch as though pulled by a string. The sound it made was somewhere between a groan and a scream, like a zombie in distress. But the sound Reese made was undeniably a scream. Her heart punched her ribs.

Lo's head came into focus. Her halo of curly blond hair shot out at weird angles, like an angelic Medusa.

"Fuck, Reesy, you scared me. What are you doing here?"

"Are you absolutely fucking with me right now? What am *I* doing here? Oh, nothing, I just flew back from New York to see if my sister had died in my apartment."

"That's a little... extreme. I was just napping." Lo stretched her arms over her head and let out a lioness yawn.

"A thirteen-hour nap? Where you couldn't hear the door or your phone ringing? Where you didn't wake up once? Judith said she's been trying to get in since late morning."

"I guess I was tired. I told Judith I was going to sleep today. We had a wild canasta night, her friends are so much fun."

"So, you're sticking with that? You were tired so you took a coma nap?"

"Fine, Reese, I took a few sleeping pills because I haven't been sleeping well lately and I used a set of your earplugs. You know how Judith loves to sing in the mornings."

"What pills?"

"Why does that matter?"

"You know why."

"This is not a big de—"

Reese was on her way to the medicine cabinet above the bathroom sink before Lo finished her sentence.

"Reese, wait." Lo's footsteps pounded behind her.

Reese didn't pause. And she didn't need to look far, a bottle of melatonin sat on the edge of the sink. Reese heard a strangled sound fill the small bathroom, echoing off the tiles. It sounded happy. Her face felt wet and the sound was her own distorted laughter. Full and delirious.

"Melatonin, really? That's basically a vitamin, Lo. I

can't believe you slept through Judith's panic because of a little melatonin."

———

REESE AND LO sat under a blanket on the couch and watched the sunrise over the balcony.

"I can't stand Judith." Reese let her head drop back on the couch and she stared at the trowel marks in the ceiling as though it was the night sky.

"I think Judes means well. I know you're upset because she messed up your time with Arden and I get that, but it's really not her fault. She was worried about me. I'm sorry she got you to come back to Chicago. I was the irresponsible one."

"No, it's not that. I don't care about leaving New York early. You're my priority and it's definitely better this way. Probably. I mean it was always going to end."

"Ok," Lo said slowly, each letter like its own word. "What are you so upset with Judes about then?"

"Can you stop calling her Judes?"

"I can but I don't think I will. You should be calling her that too, I know she's asked you to. But seriously, why are you angry?"

The back of the couch dipped where Lo's elbow came to rest on it, her body angled toward Reese.

Why was she so angry? All she knew was that the anger was a pit of lava in her stomach in need of a sacrifice to placate it.

"It's her—her unprovoked generosity. It's intrusive and out of control."

"Ok, so, you're complaining about her caring about you

as though that's not the thing we all want most in the world."

"She doesn't care about me." Reese pulled the gray blanket up to her shoulders. "She's invasive. Like those beetles and I'm a suburban maple tree."

"That's...oddly specific. And I don't think you mean that."

"I do mean it. She just inserts herself and ruins my life."

"Here's what I think. I think old Reese who never left this apartment might have meant that, but I think Arden chiseled away at the stone around your heart and now it's cracking like some sort of geode and you're scared it's going to be beautiful."

"I need you to stop talking to me like an Instagram horoscope."

"Fine, but those are another thing I really wish you'd give a chance instead of dismissing."

"Then how would you torture me?"

"I've got a few ideas. Just off the top of my head, and I am still a bit groggy, I'm thinking we should get you back out there. You know, once we finish excavating your little gem of a heart and brushing away all the debris. Unless you're maybe feeling like you're ready to get right back on a plane to New York?"

"I'm not going to New York. I'm never leaving my apartment again if I can help it."

"Ok, I guess we'll start there."

THE COFFEE WAS TAKING FOREVER. Lo had surprised her with the coffee pot she wanted and now Reese was stuck watching each individual drop sift through to the carafe like a saline drip.

"It's slow as shit, huh?"

Reese banged her knee on the counter as she spun around. Her hand went to her chest to hold her heart in place. "You scared me!"

"Sorry, but this is what you get for never having anyone around. You think humans are ghosts."

"I think this is what I get for having a sister who floats instead of walks."

Lo hopped up onto the counter, something Reese had been asking her not to do for going on three decades. She'd accepted that she'd lost the battle and the war on that one. She still cringed as Lo's heels kicked out a beat on the cabinets—she'd wipe them down later.

"Now that I have your attention, let's figure out how you can make things up and get your girl back."

"What are you talking about? I don't have a girl. I had a fling on a work trip and it ran its course."

"It ran its course or you messed it up?"

"It's actually illegal to interrogate me about feelings before coffee. And why would you think *I* messed it up?"

She had, of course, but that Lo would jump to that was insulting. Reese had cared too much and Arden had rejected her for it, why couldn't she ever learn that lesson? It was always better to be alone. No one could hurt you if you kept your door locked.

"Come on, Reese. You were wild about her. What happened?"

"I never said I was wild about her." Reese crossed her arms over her chest as the coffee continued its water torture drip.

"You said you liked her. That she got you. You spent days and nights with her. That, babe, is you being wild about her."

"Don't call me babe."

"Ok, babe."

"Fine. We had an argument at her launch. I spilled her drink on her and then after we switched clothes, she told me to leave."

"Back up. She told you to leave because you spilled her drink on her? Was it an accident? I didn't realize she was so uptight."

"It wasn't technically an accident."

"Say more."

"Her agent, Sophia, was being a jerk. She's always hard on Arden about needing to make things up for mistakes when she was drinking. She puts so much pressure on her to be perfect and Arden just believes it. I mean this woman scheduled her book launch at a bar. There was this whole cocktail menu. For a newly sober person. I saw Sophia give her a drink that looked like alcohol. I was trying to warn her before she drank any."

"That sounds reasonable. But you warned her by dumping the drink on her dress."

"No, that part was the accident."

"Ok, so why did she tell you to leave?"

"A lot of reasons. You know how stressful I find parties?"

Lo nodded.

"So, there's that—I wasn't exactly thrilled to be there. I mean, I was happy for her and I wanted to be there for her, but I also didn't *want* to be there."

"Right, so, you at every event. Go on."

"And she had asked me to stop making such a big deal about drinking and the bar and her jerk agent. Basically, she wanted me to trust her to take care of herself."

"Ah."

"Ah? Ah, what?"

"Nothing, please, go on." Lo made a sweeping gesture with her arm.

"Fine, but we're circling back to that 'Ah' later."

Lo gave her a little salute and motioned for her to continue.

"Anyway, after the drink spilled—"

"After you spilled her drink."

"Ok fine, after *I* spilled her drink on her and ruined her dress, I offered to trade outfits."

"Ok, I think I get it. And I'm finally understanding why you got home in a ruined dress. I can't believe you wore a dress for her. In public."

"Please don't remind me."

"But Reesy. If she's worth wearing a ruined dress for, when you usually wouldn't be caught dead in a non-ruined dress, even if it was black and covered in studs, then I think she'd be worth going after."

"I told you, Lo. It was always temporary. She made that clear. Now I just need to wait for the money for the project to come through so I can pay off rehab for you and then I can put this all behind me."

"Sure, great plan. Just forget what it felt like to be happy. There's only one problem though."

"Ok, what's the *one* problem?"

"Rehab is already paid off, so you're going to have to find something else to do with the money."

"What do you mean it's paid off? Where did you get that money from? I don't want you owing someone who could take advantage of you later."

"Whoa, relax. And thanks for the vote of confidence. I found this sobriety scholarship program. I wrote an essay and they picked me. Simple. I can take care of things too, Reese."

"How long ago did you win it?"

"A few weeks?"

"And you let me stay in New York anyway? You knew I only took that job to cover bills."

"I guess I wanted to do you a favor by letting you live a little."

REESE DID her best to avoid Lo for the rest of the day, she wasn't sure she could handle another bout of honesty. After lunch, she had shut herself in her room to rest. She counted the lines on her bedroom ceiling for the hundredth time as sleep remained just out of reach. The cold of the bed next to her made its way to her chest when she thought about Arden in New York, probably not thinking about her at all.

A light knock at the door pulled her out of her restless state. Maybe Lo had gone out and forgotten to take her keys. But at that moment she didn't care who was at the door. Reese would sign for 100 certified letters if it meant she didn't have to spend another minute in that bed alone with her thoughts.

JUDITH LOOKED the oldest Reese had ever seen her standing under the fluorescent hallway lights, her gray hair a chaotic scribble.

"Hi, Judith, is everything ok?"

"Yes, dear, everything's fine. I wanted to apologize for panicking yesterday. I know I messed up your trip."

"That's ok." Reese shoved her hands in her jacket

pockets and clenched them into fists as she looked around the room.

Judith's shoulders dropped a few inches as she sighed. "I was worried you'd never speak to me again, and just when we were getting close."

Had Reese missed them getting close? Judith's eyes shone with tears. Reese reached out, the wool poncho Judith was wearing was soft beneath her palm as she awkwardly patted her shoulder. "Of course not. We're still... close. I know you were looking out for Lo and I really appreciate that. She means the world to me."

Judith nodded and gave Reese a sad smile before grabbing Reese's arms and pulling her into a crushing hug like they were swing dancing.

Reese felt trapped as she tried not to move in Judith's grip. How was she so strong? Maybe Judith would release her if she stayed very still. "The plants look great, too." Reese choked out. "And really, thanks for caring for Lo."

"Anytime, you're my girls. Both of you."

"Right."

Judith released her and took a step back into the hallway. Reese placed a hand on the doorway as she blinked the floating black spots from her vision.

"Hey Judith," Reese forced out in a rush. If she didn't ask now she never would.

"Can you please call me Judes, dear?"

"Ok," Reese nodded once definitively. She could give her this. "Judes?"

"Yes?"

"Why do you care?"

"What do you mean?" Judith's nose scrunched beneath the bridge of her readers.

"Why do you care about me? Why do you care about us

—me and Lo?" The last part of her question came out in a whisper, the rising tide of emotion crashed in her chest, the water level a bit higher with each breath.

She gestured to the kitchen where Lo hummed softly as she waited for the kettle to boil. Her sister leaned against the counter twirling her hair like she always did when she was tired. Her soft flannel pajama pants and oversized t-shirt made her look small—she could have been a kid again—right after their mom left. Reese felt that same ripped open sensation, like a tornado had torn through the center of her chest.

Judith must have been talking because she seemed to be wrapping up, a warm smile crinkling the corners of her eyes. "It's simple, really, I like you. Now, I'm going to let you girls get some rest. I'll check on you tomorrow." Judith gave a little wave as she turned toward her apartment. Tears burned hot trails down Reese's face before she'd even secured the chain. She desperately needed some sleep so she could stop feeling so much.

TWENTY-TWO

The brass bell over the door of DeVines on Michigan Avenue chimed as Reese entered. The space was small and humid, lined with long low shelves covered in plants. Something had broken in her since she'd been back from New York. Much to her dismay she now found herself restless if she didn't leave her apartment at least every other day. She found herself searching for small, meaningless errands like the one she was currently on to buy Judith a thank you plant.

One wall of the shop was all windows dotted with hanging plants. The spring sun streamed in, warming the space and knocking the breath clear out of her. For a moment she could have been in Arden's apartment, pressed up against the glass as she—

"Can I help you, miss?" The young woman was wearing jeans and a denim shirt with the sleeves rolled up to reveal a jungle of tattoos.

Reese didn't love being called miss but at least this twenty-year-old hadn't ma'am-ed her. "I'm looking for something low maintenance as a thank you for a friend. She took care of my succulents while I was away, and I think she kind of liked it."

Reese stopped talking, feeling a little stunned but the sheer volume of information she'd just given to a stranger, basically unprompted. She needed to cut back on her time with Judith immediately. If Lo wanted to hang out they could do it somewhere other than her apartment.

"Sure, we definitely have what you need. What size were you thinking?"

"Just regular plant size, I think. Something I can carry though. I have a bit of a walk."

"Ok, we have these Aloe plants that have been really popular." Reese followed her over to a row of bright green and white speckled plants poking up out of terracotta pots the size of teacups. Had plants always been adorable? It seemed like they'd gotten cuter since they became Instagram influencers. "But if you're looking for something fun and a little strange, we just got these Venus Fly Traps the other day."

"I didn't realize this was a little shop of horrors."

"What?"

"Nothing. I'll take one of each." One uncomfortable joke was all it took for Reese to hit her quota for interacting with others.

Lo WAS on the couch watching Netflix. She refused to sync her headphones to the television which meant Reese spent a lot of time blocking out reality shows and Judith's singing these days.

She headed across the room to grab her headphones but the noise stopped abruptly.

Lo was turned toward her on the couch. "What do you have there?"

Reese set the brown cardboard holder on the coffee table and took out the plants to show Lo. "I thought it would be nice to get Judith a plant to thank her and give her something to do, so I got her this," she said, gesturing to the aloe.

"And who's that monster plant for?"

"Me."

"Perfect. I was worried you were going soft. You keep leaving your apartment and caring about other people."

Reese rolled her eyes at her sister. "I better go drop this off."

"Actually, speaking of reluctantly caring about people, have you called Arden?"

"Why would I call Arden? She told me to leave."

"Because you didn't want to leave? Because you can still fix it."

"There's nothing to fix. I can't keep talking about this." Reese picked up the plant, cupping her hands against the smooth terracotta pot.

Lo grabbed her wrist gently. Her eyes looked like the sky before a storm. She looked away. Reese had always had trouble seeing her sister upset.

"Reese, look at me. You can't just ignore things you don't want to deal with."

"That's where you're wrong, Lo. I absolutely can. People do it all the time."

"Fine, but you shouldn't do it this time. Not with her. I could hear your excitement anytime her name came up on our calls. Hell, you even called me when you were in New York. It was like a flame lit inside of you when you met her. You tried new things. You explored, sort of. Even now that you're back you're not the same. You just went to a store and bought a gift for Judes. Could you have imagined doing that a month ago?"

She couldn't. She couldn't even explain why she was doing it now. But this was all she had, buying gifts for Judith and trying to get on with her life. Staying busy until she didn't need a constant distraction just to make it through the days. Even thinking about Arden made her chest feel like a black hole collapsing in on itself. Was that how black holes worked? Or maybe they just pulled in all the brilliant light around them and extinguished it. The "this is why we can't have nice things" of the universe.

"Why can't I just go back to being alone and happy?"

"Because you weren't happy. You were just alone."

"I need you to be a little less honest here, Lo." Reese couldn't blink back the tears fast enough.

SOMETHING LARGE BOUNCED on the bed next to her and startled Reese awake.

"Reese, wake up!"

She pulled a pillow over her head; maybe if she blocked out Lo she would go away.

"I mean it. I brought coffee. It's time to make a plan before you go into work mode and spend the next 10 hours pretending everything is fine."

"Everything would be fine if you weren't inches from my face right now."

The cool air hit her face as Lo pulled the pillow away and tossed it to the foot of the bed. "I've given you a week and you're miserable. I don't know Arden, but I do know she's the best thing that ever happened to you. I'm not going to sit back and watch you ruin your life because you sure as hell didn't sit back when I was ruining mine."

"This isn't the same. I can't make her want me. I can't make our time together mean something." Reese's voice was climbing higher and higher, to its most dramatic register, grating even to her own ears but she couldn't help it. She felt overwhelmed and because she couldn't think of what else to do about it, she'd settle for whining.

"But I think you owe it to yourself to try. Call her. Text her. Email her. See if it meant something to her. Hell, write her a letter. Just do something, Reese." Lo leaned over Reese and grabbed her phone off the nightstand.

"Well, I have been thinking about something."

"Ok... something. That sounds promising. Tell me what you're thinking." Lo was nodding like she was trying to build momentum for this something plan.

"Arden's going to be in Chicago this weekend, signing books at a conference."

"Cool. I like that you checked her schedule. That's promising."

"Why does it seem like you already knew that?" Reese raised an eyebrow at Lo who was keeping her face carefully innocent.

"I googled her. So how are you going to get her back?"

Reese unlocked her phone and pulled up her notes app. "I didn't want to make a big deal out of it in case it doesn't work out, but I was thinking I could go to her reading and talk to her after."

Lo glanced at the list on Reese's phone, though "list" is generous for a single bullet point that says "go to conference". She sighed so hard her hair looked like it was near a wind machine. A second later a pillow hit Reese smack in the face. "That's not a grand gesture, Reese. That's just showing up to an event."

"Ok, ok. Can you help me think of something better?" Reese opened a new note and handed her phone to Lo.

"Of course. It's a low bar because literally anything is better than your plan."

"I can't believe you got that entire tart and you're not even going to give me a piece when it's my favorite. I left my apartment for you. I stood *in line* at a bakery."

"Reesy, how would it look if I show up to canasta night with dessert and a piece is missing?" As the elevator climbed, Lo moved the box to her free hand, holding it by the red and white string away from Reese.

"I think Judes would forgive me for a bite."

"Maybe you should just come to play cards instead of spending another night by yourself."

"I told you, I'm putting the finishing touches on my plan to get Arden back."

"I think it's really sweet that you're writing her a book."

"I just hope she can see past how bad it is."

"There's nothing to see past, Reesy. Don't be so hard on yourself. You're great. She'd be a fool not to want you."

"Did you just call me a fool?" A voice from around the corner that sounded just like Arden's stopped Reese dead in her tracks.

"Come on." Lo looped her free arm through Reese's and half dragged her around the corner.

There in front of her apartment sat Arden on top of the same gray scarf they'd used for their Statue of Liberty picnic.

Reese stopped short, she felt weightless like she was watching the scene from an observation deck. Arden looked perfect, her long dark hair in a bun. A white dress shirt and jeans that looked suspiciously like the outfit she's walked away from Reese in. Surely she didn't come all this way to return her clothes, right? "Hi." Reese opened her mouth to say more but she knew the lilt of hope in her voice had already given her away.

"Hi, I hope you're hungry." Arden gestured to the food around her like she was showcasing a feast on a gameshow.

Reese held back a laugh as she took in the spread. A single seltzer and two dixie cups. Tiny bottles of tabasco sauce. A thimble of olives. "You look like a giant."

"Thanks, Reese, you look great too." Arden stood and took a step toward her.

Reese hesitated. She wanted to touch Arden, make sure she was really there in her dim apartment hallway but she'd been wrong about Arden's intentions before. Her heart ached when she thought about it, but she smiled slightly anyway. "No, I just mean, why is everything so tiny? It's like a cheese board for fairies."

"Well, I had to fit it in my carry on."

"You took a picnic through airport security?"

"I did. They searched it twice, but cheese isn't an illicit substance."

"Should it be though? I guess that explains why all the bottles are so small."

"Yeah, they're really serious about the liquid limits."

"You know we have seltzer in Chicago, right?" Reese's surprised laugh bubbled up before she could stop it.

"I honestly wasn't sure what was happening in this part of the country." Arden took another step forward and placed her hand on Reese's hip. "But I also knew I wasn't stopping anywhere on my way to you. Reese, I'm so sorry. I acted like it was nothing. Like we were nothing. But you were never nothing to me."

Arden's hand on her hip was the warmest touch Reese had ever felt. Like finding a campfire after being lost in the woods for days. Her touch was hope and a second chance you'd given up on. It was a rescue when she'd least expected it.

She pulled Arden toward her. She felt like she'd been waiting her whole life to hear those words. Waiting her whole life to feel that way about someone back. "No, I'm sorry," she whispered into Arden's hair. "I should have backed off when you asked. I know you don't need anyone to take care of you."

"I don't, but I also really missed it. I was so set on not needing anyone to take care of me that I didn't stop to consider how it actually felt. I just knew I had something to prove."

"But not to me."

"No, not to you."

A throat cleared behind them. Reese had completely forgotten Lo was there, witnessing all of this. She was suddenly deeply grateful for Judes's rowdy card night.

"Arden, this is my sister Lo. Lo, Arden."

"It's great to meet you. Sorry, I've got to run—it's canasta night and the crowd Judes rolls with can get pretty wild." Lo turned to Reese. "I'll just crash at her place after. I'm sure Arden's exhausted from her flight. I assume you'll want to get to bed early and I'd hate to disturb you."

Reese could feel her face burning. No one was quite as adept at horrifying her as her sister. "Subtle, Lo. Have fun tonight."

"Well, you two enjoy this." Lo stepped gingerly over the picnic and placed the bakery box down in the center of it.

"Wait."

Lo froze midstep. "Is that why you bought my favorite dessert. Did you know about this?"

"I'm surprised you didn't realize it sooner. A fruit tart is a deeply weird thing to bring to a card game."

"I was actually kind of stunned you weren't home. When Lo said she could get you out of the apartment I didn't believe her."

Reese looked back and forth between the pair in confusion, her brows knit together. "I go out more now. But how—"

"I asked David for her number. When you disappeared during the launch I knew I'd messed up. I went straight to your hotel after, but you were already gone. So, I had to get creative." She gestured to the tiny picnic behind her.

"But why are you in the hallway? Did the key I left you not work?" Lo asked.

"I didn't try the key." Arden turned back toward Reese. "I realized going into the apartment when you weren't expecting me would probably feel like a violation. So, I decided to make the most of this very romantic corridor."

"It's perfect." Reese brought her lips to Arden's, savoring the taste of vanilla and cinnamon as tears burned her eyes. She broke their kiss and unlocked the door before grabbing two corners on the scarf and dragging it all inside like a reverse of the tablecloth trick. "But inside might be a bit more private."

Arden closed the door and Reese pressed her into it, kissing her hard, kissing her like she had everything and nothing to make up for. Kissing her like all was forgiven. But she'd still spend every day making Arden feel trusted and appreciated and loved. Reese broke their kiss and rested her forehead against Arden's. She drew a deep breath, it was the first time since New York that she felt like she could breathe, that she didn't feel restless.

"How long can you stay?" She whispered, her lips brushing against Arden's with each syllable.

"As long as you want." Arden reached forward and grabbed Reese's hips pulling her forward.

She'd been back at her apartment for days but finally she felt home.

EPILOGUE

SIX MONTHS LATER

Reese set the heavy cardboard box on the floor and pulled her wild hair into a short ponytail. Was her apartment even big enough for all this stuff? No, not her apartment. Their apartment.

She turned to Arden, who was shotgunning a seltzer. "Is that the last of it, Denny?"

"Yup, that's it. I still can't believe I'm letting you call me that." Arden stepped behind Reese and slid her hands into the front pockets of Reese's jeans.

"It really hasn't grown on you? Because last night in your apartment you didn't seem to mind." Reese leaned back against Arden and swayed a bit. A thirteen hour drive plus unloading a moving truck and she was glad she had someone to hold her up. Why had she let Lo talk her into dinner tonight?

"Well, I was very emotional saying goodbye to that window. Plus, you get a pass with nicknames just like with everything else, but if David or Lo start calling me Denny, I'm calling the whole thing off."

"Yeah, that's fair." Reese looked at the stacks of cardboard boxes around the room.

"I can't believe you're finally here."

"Babe, I've been here most of the last six months. I basically only went back to New York to water my plants."

"I know. But now you're *here* here. No more suitcases or countdowns."

"Right, no more suitcases or countdowns. Unless we take a trip." Arden's dark eyes glimmered playfully in the bright summer sun coming in through the windows.

"Don't push it." Reese smirked. "How did Sophia take it?"

"She was against me leaving New York. We had lunch last week and she sort of hinted she wouldn't be my agent anymore if I went through with it. Something about the midwest being a dead zone."

"Do you think she was serious?"

"Who knows, I think it could have been a bluff. But I'm serious about it. I actually wrote up a contract termination request."

"Oh." Reese tempered her excitement, holding back a grin. Sophia had meant a lot to Arden for a long time. "Are you going to send it?"

Arden nodded, biting her lower lip. "I sent it from the truck this morning, somewhere in Ohio."

"I can't believe you didn't tell me! How do you feel?"

"I feel free and happy and a little concerned about what we're going to do with all these plants. And all my books."

Tall stacks of boxes dotted the living room and kitchen like roman columns. Hopefully, they were just as stable.

"Buy more shelves, I guess. But let's worry about that later. I'm proud of you."

"Thanks, babe. I'm proud of me, too. But I do think we

should worry about my stuff *now,* seeing as your sister will be here in a few hours and the apartment looks like a failed game of Tetris."

Reese turned in Arden's embrace until they were facing. She raised her tired arms and laced them around her neck. "About that. Let's cancel."

"We can't cancel, Reese. I want her to like me."

"She already loves you." Reese kissed Arden once, then again. "Didn't she ask you to go to her meditation recovery meeting with her this weekend?"

"Yeah, but she was just being nice."

"Lo's definitely the nice one, but not about sobriety. If she invited you, she wants you there, I promise."

"Ok, but still we should get some of these boxes taken care of." Arden half-turned from Reese, knitting her brows together as she took in the stacks of boxes again.

It was pretty overwhelming. Reese had gotten better about dealing with unpleasant stuff over the last few months, but unpacking was a new circle of hell paralleled only by the chaos of clutter. Leaving the room would help. They hadn't stacked any boxes in the bathroom, right?

"I think we deserve a break, don't you? My arms are too tired to unpack."

"That's fair. Do you want to take a nap before dinner? I can get started on organizing."

"I think I need a shower first."

Arden pulled Reese's hair down and ran her hands through it, leaving the short strands chaotic. She should have never let Arden convince her to cut it into a bob. She felt like a mad scientist most of the time, hopped up on static electricity.

"Thanks Denny, that's helpful."

Arden gave her hair one last ruffle. "Ok, go. I'll shower after you."

A HOT SHOWER after an exhausting day was more delicious than any meal Reese could imagine. It was definitely better than the road trip snacks they'd had, full of stale trail mix and fruit leather. The water ran over her tight shoulders, unwinding the knots from the grueling drive and the six days it took to ford Pennsylvania and Ohio, where she felt her spirit die of dysentery.

She reached up to wash her hair and her arms fell back to her sides in protest. She would definitely be getting Arden an e-reader for her birthday. Never again would she move 20 boxes of books down from a 5th floor walkup.

The glob of shampoo she'd gotten on her hair shifted unpleasantly. Should she just lean her head back to rinse it out and go on with her life? Probably not the best look for company later.

"Denny?"

"Yeah, babe." Arden's voice was closer than she expected and sleepy sounding. She'd probably laid down in bed the second Reese left the room.

"I think your books broke my arms, will you help me wash my hair?"

A few seconds later, the bathroom door creaked open and the shower curtain slid aside. Arden quirked an eyebrow at her. "Really, Reese, you need my help with your hair? Did the boxes really hurt you that badly, or is this a euphemism?"

"Well, they hurt my pride when I wasn't able to carry more than you. I thought I was the strong one."

"You're the only one who thought that, babe." Arden

pulled the faded Great Lakes Swimmers t-shirt that she'd stolen from Reese over her head and dropped it on the floor. She slowly unbuttoned her jeans and held Reese's gaze as she slid them down her legs.

"It's starting to feel like you have something in mind besides helping me."

"Does it have to be mutually exclusive?" Arden dangled her bra from her fingertips and let it fall next to her feet. The light coming through the bathroom window trailed across her skin as she stood in her cotton, distinctly not date underwear. She'd never looked more beautiful.

Arden's hair fell in waves around her shoulders as she let it down. She raked a hand through it, pushing it to one side as she stepped into the water.

She massaged the shampoo into Reese's hair, her fingers trailing gently in concentric circles. Reese couldn't hold back her sigh, and the sound of it filled the small room.

"I love getting good reviews like that." Arden's lips ghosted across Reese's and then disappeared. Arden placed a finger under her chin, tilting her head back into the warm water.

Too soon, Arden took a step back and Reese opened her eyes, blinking away the water and adjusting to the bright light of day.

"That was nice."

"I got that impression."

"Good."

Reese took a step forward and placed her hands on Arden's hips closing the distance between them and bringing their lips together. Arden deepened the kiss and leaned into it for a moment. She couldn't get sidetracked. Company would arrive soon.

She forced herself to pull away and looked into Arden's

eyes. They grew darker by the moment, like night taking over the sunset sky as Reese sank to her knees.

Arden's fingers returned to her hair. "What are you doing? I thought you were tired."

"Just my arms. You know I like getting good reviews too." She nudged Arden's knee, encouraging her as she placed her leg over Reese's shoulder.

She placed a slow kiss just below Arden's belly button. The groan that followed and the sound of the hand smacking against the tile wall for balance sent a shiver through Reese, even with the hot water sluicing down her back.

"Welcome home," Reese mumbled against Arden's hip before her lips journeyed lower. And the taste of Arden was just that: home.

Reese braced a hand against Arden's ass, lifting her leg higher as she made soft, lazy circles around her clit with her tongue. Arden's hand in her hair gripped so tightly that she couldn't have explored lower if she wanted to. Instead, Reese listened to the white noise of the rushing water and Arden's breaths that crashed like waves.

"Oh my god, Reese, I can't hold myself up, I'm going to —" a long moan cut off Arden's words. Her body went rigid. Reese held still as Arden rode out her orgasm, placing one last kiss before she lowered Arden's leg down slowly.

She reached up and disentangled Arden's hand from her hair and stood up.

"Sorry."

"Don't be, but I think all the soap's out now. Do you want my help showering?"

"If I say yes, I think we'll run out of warm water before I get clean."

Reese gave Arden a quick kiss and stepped out of the shower. "I'll get dressed and clean up the apartment a bit."

ARDEN WALKED into the living room and sat down on the couch. Reese had made a path through the boxes that reminded her of an ant farm. It was technically possible to get from one end of the apartment to the other, but there were definitely some dead ends.

"Come here." Arden held her arms out and Reese stepped forward until Arden's legs were between hers.

"Remind me why we can't just be alone tonight?"

"Because Lo wanted to do a housewarming dinner, and she sent me 23 emails about it. And I really want her to like me."

"I told you already, she likes you. We can blame it on me. She will 100% believe that I don't want to see people."

"You were in New York for a week and a half helping me pack. You really don't want to see anyone?"

"Ugh, fine. I guess it would be nice to see her and make sure she's alive."

Arden pulled her phone from the pocket of her jeans. "Well, you've got an hour before you have to see anyone else. Do you want some time alone or can I make the most of it? You disappeared from the shower before I had my chance."

"Interesting. I remember you asking me to leave." Reese tilted her head to one side and furrowed her brow.

"It's so cute when you're wrong."

Reese crossed her arms and moved to take a step back in protest, but Arden caught her hips and pulled her forward until Reese was straddling her lap.

"That's better, now I've got you right where I want

you." Arden kissed Reese hard, nipping at Reese's bottom lip. Reese parted her lips and as their tongues met, she rocked her hips. Arden rose slightly to meet her and Reese groaned against the friction.

There was something about fully clothed make outs that got her hotter than anything else. Arden's hand snuck under her t-shirt and she cupped Reese through her bra and squeezed. Reese's breath was loud in her own ears as she pressed closer to Arden.

"Want to take these off?" Arden flicked open the button of Reese's jeans and lowered the zipper in a fluid motion.

"Let's leave them on."

"Ok." Arden bit Reese's neck as she slid her hand into Reese's underwear.

Something clattered behind the couch. Reese shot up pulling Arden's hand away as she looked over her shoulder to see what the noise was. Maybe a box just fell?

"Sorry dears, don't mind me! I just need to plug my crock pot in, Lo put me on appetizer duty and I'm making my famous spinach artichoke dip. I'll just take this to the kitchen and then be out of your way. I'm not looking."

Judith loudly hummed 'la la la' as though noise would somehow help her see less. She let out a surprised "ope" as another box crashed to the floor.

Reese stared wide eyed at Judith. She tried to scramble up to standing but Arden held her in place. "It's ok babe. I'm sure she didn't see anything."

"She *shouldn't* have seen anything because this is not her apartment and I know I locked the door."

"Hey Judes," Arden called sweetly, "was the door locked?"

"It was."

"I thought you gave your key to Lo?" Reese tried to cut back the exasperation in her voice.

"I did! I had to use the extra key I had made for emergencies. It was a little sticky, but I figured you weren't home because the chain wasn't on."

"I told you we need to always use the chain," Reese whispered to Arden.

"Babe, it's ok. She didn't see anything. Aren't you grateful for all the boxes of books now?"

"Do you mind if I move some boxes around in here so I can plug this in?" Judith yelled from the kitchen.

"I'll be right there." Reese tried to stand again, but Arden shook her head once firmly.

Reese settled back down.

"Oh, don't bother getting up, two minutes and I'll be out of your hair. It will be like I was never even here! I'll just slide this over—" The sound of another box falling cut off her statement.

"My body is telling me she's very much here."

"I know, babe."

Judith crashed her way back to the door. "Ok dears, I'll see you in a bit!" She said cheerily as the door shut behind her. Reese listened for the click of the lock but didn't hear it.

"Ok, now where were we?"

"We can't. We probably only have five minutes before she realizes she forgot something and bursts back in."

"Look at me." Arden brought her hands up to Reese's face and caught her gaze. "Let's make the most of our time alone together."

THANK YOU!

Thank you so much for reading my first full-length novel Must Love Silence! As an indie author your support means everything to me! If you want to know about what's coming next, including Just My Type, a funny and sexy lesbian vampire romance co-write with Bryce Oakley you can sign up for my newsletter here!

CONTINUE READING FOR A
PREVIEW OF LUCY'S NOVEL NO
STRINGS

NO STRINGS

a lesbian romance

Lucy Bexley

SYNOPSIS

Fun is the one thing **Elsie Webb** takes seriously. Though she'd be having a lot more of it if Haelstrom Media paid her enough to actually get out of debt. She's determined to hold out on contract negotiations for her kids' television show Fangley Heights until she gets what she deserves. There's only one problem, the head of the network just died and left her future more uncertain than ever.

Forty-eight hours and one funeral—that's all **Jones Haelstrom** has to get through before she can return to her life in LA that's as ordered and sparse as an IKEA showroom. When she steps in as CEO of her father's media company, Elsie Webb is her first problem to deal with. Elsie ends up challenging Jones in ways she never could have predicted, starting with an attraction neither can avoid.

As their attraction teeters on the edge of something more both agree to keep it casual. A no-strings agreement and disclosure to HR should be enough to keep things between Jones and Elsie from getting tangled, right?

CHAPTER ONE

ELSIE

W as hitting someone with a puppet technically assault? Elsie's mind said yes, but her heart— and hopefully a jury—said no. She didn't want to risk hurting the star of the show, even if he was made of felt. Not to mention, that bundle of fabric and stuffing kept a roof over her head. Elsie grimaced. She didn't really think of Fangley like that—he was a more realized person than half of her colleagues.

The set of her show Fangley Heights was gearing up for a day of filming and Elsie was already nearing her limit.

"Stop trying to control the puppet. Relax. Let *it* control you."

Elsie cringed as Trey's hand came to rest on her shoulder like a small, hot pancake, lingering for a few scorching seconds before it slid off. Trey used his hypnotist's voice, something he'd learned from one of his afternoon acting workshops. Soft and wispy and boring as hell.

Elsie had to admit it was effective. Talking to Trey did make her want to pass out to escape any further interaction with him. His personality was a constant interruption. It was like he couldn't resist talking when she was trying to focus. Her entire job was to control puppets, and he was trying to make it into some kind of metaphorical, New Age thing instead of what it was: skillful manipulation. These puppets didn't even have strings.

As the nephew of the Haelstrom's second in charge, Trey was the network's golden boy even though Elsie carried the show and frankly, she was reaching her limit with being anyone's second choice. And okay, so maybe there was that one time she had insulted some 'important' sponsors by comparing their conversation to oyster crackers that have been in an old woman's purse since the Great Depression. So dry she was left choking on their dust. But still, people didn't give second chances anymore? Was it too late to stick a stipulation in her contract for next season that Trey's puppet, Smirch, would meet an untimely end? To date, giving Trey's puppet the worst possible name was her proudest accomplishment. Even if it was technically her roommate, Avery, who had come up with it during a particularly intense game of Jenga.

Elsie took a deep breath to keep from laughing at the memory of Avery knocking over the tower in exuberance when the name occurred to them. She checked her monitor as she raised her right arm over her head and above the small wall in front of her. One thing they don't tell you about puppeteering is, it makes your shoulders look great. Like seriously ripped. Well, mostly just the one shoulder, but still they should put that in the drama school brochure. Maybe she could contribute that tidbit so they'd stop asking her for money, which they absolutely knew she didn't have.

"I think if you just loosen your wrist, you could—"

Elsie sliced her gaze at Trey.

His warm whisper washed over her face and she shuddered. With her headset over her ears, she couldn't hear most of what he was saying, a small mercy, but the fact that she could see a bit of sweat on his forehead made his proximity vaguely threatening. What she'd like to do was control him. She'd donate him to Goodwill.

Elsie glanced back down at her monitor. Trey's fingers seared her skin as they wound around her wrist. His new gold watch jangled. She added 'demand a raise' to her running mental list of contract negotiation points. Elsie had a good feeling that all she had to do to get all the stipulations she wanted was to hold out for a few more days. The network would cave, she just knew it.

She took a deep breath and lowered her headset. "Are you trying to derail my entire process?"

"You just looked like you needed my help keeping this little guy steady." Trey reached up to touch Fangley. *Nobody* touched Elsie's puppet. She flicked her wrist so Fangley's hand smacked Trey's forehead before he had the chance. He blinked at her but made no move to call the authorities. So hitting someone annoying with a puppet technically wasn't assault, just as she'd suspected.

Rebecca, the showrunner, poked her head through the studio door and called Trey over. Elsie felt the tension drain out of her. Even Fangley's shoulders relaxed.

Elsie used the momentary peace to ready herself for the scene they were filming that afternoon, the one where Fangley and his cat sidekick, Ratatouille, put on way too much makeup in an attempt to fit in. The beautiful thing about the show was that its connection to reality could be tenuous as long as the bits were engaging. For example, why would a blue-tinted young vampire like Fangley and his Maine Coon sidekick think doing a full clown face of makeup would make them *less* conspicuous? Either way, she was looking forward to the arrival of Gabby, Rata-touille's handler.

The Fangley universe worked on a perfect kind of logic: very little of it.

Fangley Heights was in its third year of production. Most days Elsie couldn't believe her luck. She had picked essentially the most unemployable major, despite her father's desire for her to do something respectable. What he really meant was something with a high earning poten-tial. Her father saw money as a down payment toward happiness, but he always forgot about the mortgage. Elsie had found no correlation between respectability and the size of her bank account. Quite the opposite, actually. Besides, she literally couldn't do math or handle bills. Even calculating tips was beyond her. On the other hand, the idea of saving people made something catch in her chest. So business and medicine were out. Her father wanted her to be employable. She wanted to be happy. But on *Fangley Heights*, most days she was both. Now if only everyone she'd ever met would stop making weird jokes about her being a puppeteer. At the very least bad jokes should be original.

But there wouldn't be a job, puppeteer or otherwise, if she couldn't get next season's agreement worked out. With each contractless day she barreled closer to an uncertain future.

She'd pushed her luck in negotiations, but why shouldn't she be better compensated? Fangley was her intel-lectual property, even if Haelstrom Media owned the trade-mark. Though it felt hard to say where everything would land with that in light of Hunter Haelstrom's recent pass-ing. That little vamp went all the way back to a web series she'd done to kill the time she should have spent memorizing Hamlet in grad school. A little something productive to assuage her guilt over wasting time.

Her classmates tried to dismiss children's television as fluff, but this wasn't Punch and Judy hour. *Fangley Heights* had depth. It had whimsy with slightly charred edges. It only barely made sense. It was a show about an orphan vampire being fostered by a family in Brooklyn—a true American story. When Haelstrom Media had reached out to her just before graduation, she couldn't believe her luck. Elsie had felt so sure signing that contract would be her golden ticket, but she was young and naive. She didn't understand sub-clauses and percentages or that one paragraph they always threw in that stipulated media appearance requirements.

Maybe they'd learned their lesson after her season one sponsor disaster. She wished now she'd read that contract, committed every line to memory. Been asked to do a series of complicated crosswords before signing it. But she hadn't, because this was back when she still trusted people to do the right thing. She thought she'd pay off her loans, buy an apartment, and stop worrying about getting by. And yet, they were wrapping up season three and she was still sharing a place with Avery. Treating themselves meant the fancy two-for-one egg roll special.

Elsie was struggling, even though her character was a cultural icon to kids everywhere who were still learning to tie their shoelaces. Fangley was a celebrity. If a puppet could be a celeb. What was she saying? *Of course* a puppet could be famous. Oscar the Grouch? Rizzo? Iconic. Plus, as a nine-year-old vampire desperate to fit in, Fangley was relatable. For the pun-filled *Make-Over-Done* episode, Elsie had spent a solid week working with their local designer and props team on *Drag Fangley*, as she'd been thinking of him. He looked almost frightening this way, just this side of familiar, like a woman in a facemask. A ghoul you could trust.

Elsie studied Fangley and wondered if she should have let the costume department and designers just craft a mask for him. They had made some latex prototypes to mimic a cold cream and blush treatment, but they all looked too much like meringue, the cold cream mask crested in waves. And when Elsie had done a run-through of the scenes with Fangley and the mask, none of his expressions had been visible. Which upped the creep factor considerably past the tolerance of their kindergarten focus group.

The creation of a new Fangley had set them back several weeks and Rebecca warned they were approaching a meeting-with-the-boss level of being behind schedule. All of that was up-in-the-air now with the new boss still being uncertain. But Elsie had a good feeling about today. The "makeup" could be layered on individually to the new version of Fangley; she had the blush and eyelashes lined up on a table behind the wall of the set. Everything was ready to stick on Fangley's ghastly face. They'd be taking a Mr. Potato Head approach. There was probably a merchandising opportunity here, not that she was giving those ideas away to Haelstrom Media for free anymore. Elsie was still waiting to see any income from her point zero five percent share of sales from trademarked Fangley merchandise.

Elsie set about her pre-rehearsal routine. The choreography of puppets was intense. Like synchronized swimming, or one of those two-piece horse costumes. Reliably, Elsie was the ass of their outfit. In this week's episode, Amanda was playing Fangley's next-door neighbor and Trey was playing Fangley's nemesis, the elementary school's suspicious science teacher. A perfect role because it was easy for Elsie and Fangley to get into the mindset of hating him.

Elsie racked her body over the foam roller, extending her back and listening to it creak and pop as she raised her arms over her head. They had an area off to the side of the set for the explicit purpose of working out the kinks that came with contorting their bodies into puppeteering postures. Sometimes it took hours after a shoot for the stiffness in Elsie's torso to fade to tolerable. She brought her hands to the ground, bracing into a wheel shape. There was a whiff of the medieval about modern-day self-care; facial peels, cooking yourself in the sun, stretching your body over a cylinder until it gave way with a series of satisfying cracks. Torture therapy.

Elsie stood slowly, like she was being raised to standing. She punched in her code and freed Fangley from his case. The puppets sitting in a row in their glass enclosures, like little lockers, reminded Elsie of babies in a hospital nursery. Tempting to snatch but constantly monitored.

Elsie set Fangley on the fake stone wall as she considered his outfit. In an increasingly routine bout of interference, the network had insisted on Fangley wearing his black cape even though that made no sense if he was trying to fit in. Everyone knew Fangley preferred to only wear his cape at home, it was a comfort item, like a blanket. But there was concern from 'certain sectors of the market' that kids were forgetting that Fangley was a vampire because the show was doing too good a job of humanizing him. Even though vampires are human, technically. Though in this case, everyone's a puppet.

The door to the fake brownstone creaked open, and out stepped Trey. His conversation with Rebecca must have been brief for him to already be back on set; Elsie hadn't realized they'd finished talking already. So much for her break.

Now she was left to wonder how long Trey had been there, silently observing her? Add that to the list of things it was better to never know. Maybe the network should be more concerned about humanizing Trey.

He hopped down the stairs from the front door to the stage and clicked his heels. In her head, Elsie watched a fantasy of him slipping on a banana peel. Ah, the power of imagination.

"So are we going to do this scene, Els? I've got a good feeling about this afternoon."

"I always come to work, Trey."

"As long as you don't throw a fit about outfits again." He reached for Elsie's shoulder but pulled his hand back as though her arm had been replaced with a bear trap. So, he had the ability to read body language after all.

"Having an opinion isn't throwing a fit. Are you going to throw a fit about your lines?" Trey's secondary character, Myrtle, was slated to be roped in by Fangley to help fix his makeup disaster in time for the spelling bee.

"No self-respecting ten-year-old girl would go along with Fangley's makeover plan."

"As someone who was once a ten-year-old girl, I can confirm that they're usually not very self-respecting."

Elsie breathed a sigh of relief as the director walked onto the set. The official signal that filming was about to start. Only Trey could be less annoying playing an evil puppet named Smirch than as himself.

THEY WERE deep into filming the second scene, the one with Trey's character, when he tripped over Elsie's not-at-all outstretched leg and they had to pause for the day. As they broke and the crew brought Trey ice, Rebecca waved Elsie over to the production control room.

This would be a good opportunity to get Rebecca's advice on her contract woes. Though the way her forehead was doing a Shar-Pei impression gave Elsie pause. Maybe she could see if the props department still had some of that cold cream from *Drag Fangley* on hand.

"So, I've got some bad news." Rebecca gave her a tight smile.

"Okay." *Shit.* "Is everything alright with Fangley?"

"Yes, of course. He's a puppet." Rebecca looked at Elsie like she was ridiculous for caring about the vampire that was literally keeping them both in a job. Millions of people cared about Fangley. He even had his own fan club: The Fangers. Not a name she would have chosen, but the fanbase of five-year-olds were not to be swayed.

"I just got word from the network, and well, you're aware that Hunter Haelstrom passed away last week, right?"

"Yes, it's very unfortunate." Elsie nodded. It was one of those things that was sad in the *royal we* sense but not necessarily upsetting to her personally.

Rebecca shrugged. "He was in his 80s and never once looked me in the eye."

"Okay, so marginally sad. I assume some people are very upset. I didn't really know him, aside from the name on my check. Do you have any idea who's taking over? Have you heard anything?"

"I'm pretty sure the will named his widow. I've only met her once, at the Christmas party two years ago, but I got the sense she wasn't a fan of the work we do here on the Heights. Did you meet her there?"

"Oh, I think I was sick that day." Elsie shrugged. She probably had been sick—sick of absolutely everything going on at work. "Do you think she'll change the show? I mean, she wouldn't, right? The numbers are good and growing each year, but I don't trust Stu for a second not to try to oust us."

Rebecca raised her hands. "I don't have any information. I know these things aren't always logical. We should take every opportunity to make sure she knows how amazing this show is. And I think it's in our best interest to get this season wrapped this week even if it means spending a few nights together. I don't want Stu to see even the tiniest window to give this show to Trey."

"I don't mind pulling all-nighters, but you know I have a no-overnights-with-Trey policy." Elsie shuddered. "Besides, who will get Trey an air cast? He might even lose the leg."

"I've never met anyone who applies soccer foul performances to real life. Once I saw him get a paper cut and fall to the ground asking for stitches."

Elsie caught the gleam in Rebecca's eye. She almost never let loose on Trey. Rebecca was in her 50s and the consummate professional. At work, anyway. Rebecca at Chewy's, the bar down the street, was a delightful person to spend time hating things with.

Elsie wiped a tear of laughter from her eye and took a deep breath. She loved mean Rebecca. Was there anything more soul-nourishing than shit talk? "I'm so sad I missed that. Next time keep the camera running. We can add it to his showreel. Maybe get him some more dramatic roles."

"Noted." Rebecca's face sobered. "I think it's critical for everyone to sign and lock in their contracts. Please tell me you're not still dragging your feet on yours." Rebecca looked at Elsie like she was going to explain why she wasn't mad, just disappointed.

Elsie grimaced.

"I mean it about your contract, Elsie. You need to sign."

"Signing it is me saying it's okay to treat me this way. To underpay me while making a killing off of my ideas." Elsie's last contract draft had been an offer so laughably low that she'd used it to sop up her spilled Lucky Charms milk.

She had *created* the show, and yet every year it felt like she was begging them to pay her enough to buy fresh vegetables. The fact that an apple in Manhattan went for ten dollars was beside the point. Then again, wasn't some money better than no money at all? That's what Avery would tell her. *Just keep us in bubble bath and bubble tea, babe.* Maybe if the show went up a little and met her halfway she could consider maybe, possibly, signing her name on the dotted line. Which was always a solid line, actually.

"I know you wanted to hold out for more money, and I think they're ready to meet you at..." Rebecca glanced at her iPad. "Seven percent below your ask. I'd take it if I were you."

All wavering drained from Elsie. *Seven percent BELOW her ask?* Were they absolutely fucking with her? Last week it was five percent. She planted her feet. Absolutely fuck that. "That's a worse offer than before. How much below Trey's ask are you advising him to take?"

"Even if I had all the details, *which I don't*, you know I can't discuss the specifics of other people's contracts." Rebecca's eyes flitted to the monitor in the control room that showed Trey sitting on the floor holding ice on his ankle and scrolling through his phone.

"Right, because telling me how much I'm being screwed

would be grossly unfair to you and the network." Elsie turned to leave. She had an overwhelming desire for this day to end.

Rebecca caught her arm. "Look, just think about it, okay? This show matters so much to all of us. I don't want to see your dream crumble."

But Elsie *had* thought about it. Fangley Heights was her baby. The only thing she'd ever invested herself in fully. But if she could love something she created this much, who was to say she couldn't do it again? She thought about the notebook on her desk, full of half-finished sketches and jokes that brought tears to her eyes. That had always been her barometer for good ideas—what reaction they sparked in her. If she didn't find her own jokes funny, why would anyone else?

Elsie pushed open the door. "Trust me, Rebecca, this is far from my only dream." The door clattered behind her. If drama school had taught her anything, it was the power of a dramatic exit.

ACKNOWLEDGMENTS

G, thanks for all you do so I can write terrible jokes on the internet and also in word documents. It's a dream come true. Thanks to my dog, Copley, you were always there for me writing this book. Sometimes, like now, you were literally on top of me. My cats contributed all typos.

Bryce, thanks for all the commas, I will be selling some of them on the dark web. This is a joke because I actually can't put into words how thankful I am to you for everything. I can't wait to release our first of many co-writes soon.

S, your writing is an inspiration and your friendship is a gift. Thanks for reading this story and encouraging me. I didn't even know how much I needed your support until you offered it to me.

L.I.L.Y., you support me and everyone else. I think you're a superhero. I'm honored to be your friend/wife.

To the Dad Jobs, you are the best thing that ever happened to my writing life. You are the champs!

Sam, thanks for saving me from drowning in similes even when I couldn't save myself. (Look, no similes in that one!)

Milena, thank you so much for reading this story and catching all the things I missed and reminding me that readers don't live in my head. You are a great friend, my dude.

Anna, thanks for encouraging me to write and helping me get off the ground. I can't believe you're still putting up with me.

Amanda, you did an incredible job editing this book and I'm so glad to know you. Thanks for taking my side in the great seltzer debate and for joining twitter so I can tag you in praise and terrible jokes.

To all my twitter pals, you make my days brighter and support me at my most absurd. It is a gift I don't take for granted.

If I forgot anyone it is only because I am very tired.

Most of all, thanks to everyone reading this! None of this would be possible without your support.

ABOUT THE AUTHOR

Lucy Bexley writes romcoms where queer women trip over things and fall... in love with each other. Her stories balance laughter and love with real-world struggles such as anxiety and addiction. Lucy lives in Boston with her partner, pets, and several cases of seltzer. She's the author of best-selling sapphic romances including No Strings and Must Love Silence. When she's not writing jokes in a Word doc, she's writing them on Twitter.

www.lucybexley.com